Ruthie B. Goose
Birth of the Legend

By

Ruthie & Jeff Baker

Ruthie B. Goose – Birth of the Legend

Hardcover ISBN-978-1-60910-144-2

Paperback ISBN-978-1-60910-145-9

Printed in the United States of America.

Booklocker.com, Inc.

2010

Cover and inside art by Dan Gibson

Author photo by Paula Baker

Dedication

This book is dedicated to the people who inspire us; our family and friends.

To Paula, who served as an invaluable sounding board, supporter and editor.

To Andrew, who helped add his own brand of humor and his sunny outlook on life to this book.

To the hard working people at the Muscular Dystrophy Association (MDA) and the people they serve. We suffer with Charcot-Marie-Tooth Disorder (CMT) and have pledged to donate a portion of the proceeds from this book to MDA to help in the quest to find a cure for this and other neuromuscular diseases. $2.00 from all hardcover and $1.00 from all paperback books will go directly to Jerry's Kids.

In addition, we would like to thank Joan Feeney for her help editing this book and Dan Gibson for providing the illustrations seen on the cover and throughout the book.

We would also like to extend thanks & appreciation to the people of Wilmington, MA and the Wilmington Public Library, where we wrote this entire book.

Table of Contents

This is the story of a little bird and her big dream...

CHAPTER 1
A Very Special Day

November 18th is a very special day in our house. You see it is the birthday of our pride and joy Ruthie B. Goose. November 18th may be the day of her birth, but August 16th is the day her legend was born!

I'm her dad and this is her story.

It was a cool fall day in Central Park in the heart of New York City. The leaves had already fallen from the trees but it had not yet snowed. The blaze of colors that had decorated Central Park just a few weeks prior had given way to the grayness that comes with the arrival of winter.

Our house nestled high in an old oak tree in the middle of Central Park was in complete chaos. My wife, Mrs. B. Goose, was on pins and needles getting everything ready for the baby's arrival.

During the last few weeks all of our friends had been welcoming their bundles of joy. Not us. We were still waiting. We just continued to wait and wait for our little one to break through its shell. Each day came news of another arrival in our community. Ours was just stubborn and didn't want to hatch and join our happy home. I think little Ruthie B. was nice and comfortable there in her egg and she just wasn't ready to come out and join our world.

"Don't fret, my dear," I said to my wife as she finished making the baby's new bed in the far corner of the family room. "I know today is the day. I feel it," I said.

"You've said that every day for the past sixteen days," my wife said. "I'm getting tired of your feelings and my tushie is getting tired of sitting on that egg. The day is almost over and still nothing. I wonder what she is waiting for."

Just then, I felt a strange commotion just below me and a sudden kick to my tushie! You see, I was sitting on that egg, giving my wife a break, when I felt a little kick to my rear end. I quickly arose to see a little foot, with four perfect webbed toes, poking out of that white and brown speckled egg.

"Hurry! Hurry!" I franticly called to my wife, who was still in the other corner of the room. "It's time!!! The baby is finally here!!!"

My wife came running, faster than I had ever seen her move. She zipped left, jumped right over my favorite stool and landed right at the spot where the egg was resting.

"You were right! Today is the day! Today is the day that I become Mommy and you become Daddy. Today is truly a very special day!" my wife said.

Just how special, well we'd discover that sooner than we'd ever have dreamed.

CHAPTER 2
Spreading Her Wings

During the first year of a young bird's life they learn to do many things. They learn how to feed themselves and how to play and interact with others; however the most special thing they learn is how to fly on their own.

The most important day in every young bird's life is the first day they fly on their own. When a young bird first spreads its wings, begins to flap them up and down and leaves the ground on their own, well it's truly a momentous day. There is no feeling quite like it! Every bird remembers their first flight and Ruthie B. Goose's first time was no different. Okay, you caught me… it wasn't just different, it was historic! Ruthie's first flight was the start of something truly special, the first step in the birth of the legend.

Ruthie's first flight happened accidentally on the night of July 4th.

Central Park was crowded with birds from all over the city. Pigeons flew in from the Bronx, seagulls from Coney Island and robins from Queens. They all came to see the special fireworks display. Birds of all shapes and sizes were flocking to the park, seeking a great vantage point to view that night's spectacular fireworks show.

Since November, Ruthie B. had grown from a fuzzy little baby chick into an adventurous young girl. Her feathers filled out to a pretty snow-white, her beak was a brilliant orange-yellow (with a little brown freckle on the tip) and her wings were becoming more powerful every day. By July 4th she was able to leave our tree with our help, but still couldn't fly on her own. This wasn't a result from a lack of trying.

"Like this Daddy?" she asked as she spread her wings as wide open as she could.

"Yes, just like that little one," I said.

"And do I flap them up and down together like this or one at a time just like this?" she questioned as she spun herself quickly to the left losing her balance and falling on her side.

"That's enough practicing for today dear," my wife said trying to control her giggling. "Why don't you go out to the limb and your father will take you down to watch the fireworks show with your friends?"

Ruthie hated having to be helped up and down our tree but her desire to see the fireworks show and spend some time with her friends far outweighed her desire to keep learning how to fly.

"Let's go Daddy. Those fireworks are coming soon and I want to catch up with the guys," Ruthie said.

"Ok little one. Hold on tight," I said as she hopped on my back. "You are getting a little heavy for your old dad to be picking you up."

"Oh Daddy, stop being so silly, I'm the same size today as I was yesterday," she said.

"Yes, but I'm a day older," I said.

We slowly glided down to the brick wall behind our tree. I dropped her off and made my way back home.

"Have a good time. Mommy and I are going to watch the show from our branch. I'll be back to pick you up after the show."

CHAPTER 3
It All Started With a Big Bang

R uthie watched as I made my ascent back up to the tree and home. She casually turned and began making her way towards her usual meeting place. To her dismay, she saw that her whole gang was already there. She suddenly realized that meant that they had all seen her dad drop her off.

"Still catching rides on 'Air Dad' I see," said her pal Marty Beekman, who everyone called The Answer. Marty somehow knew the answer to every question and was never too shy about providing it. Marty is a gangly seagull with a long thin neck, ruffled feathers and a know-it-all smirk. Marty was the first in Ruthie's group to fly on his own and considered himself quite an expert flyer.

"Ruthie, when are you going to learn how to fly on your own?" asked a pretty little sparrow named KT. KT is the smallest of Ruthie's friends. She is quiet and always very polite but most importantly she is Ruthie's best friend.

"We've all been flying on our own for more than a month now," she commented. "Even Evan," she said, in a whisper, from the side of her mouth.

"Yes, I know. You all know how to fly: you, The Answer, Backwards Bob, Perfect Jen and even Evan, the Incredible Hawk boy. But not me, I'm still catching rides with my mom and dad. Don't you think I know that? It's not like I haven't been trying to learn! I've been practicing every day for the past four weeks but nothing seems to be happening. I don't think I'll ever learn how to fly," said Ruthie.

"Hey Penguin, did you just fly in? I must have missed you soaring in," said Perfect Jen. Perfect Jen is a stunningly perfect red cardinal. Perfect Jen liked to call Ruthie "Penguin" because she knew it got under Ruthie's skin. Being called a short stubby flightless bird just really bothered Ruthie but she just chose to grin and bear Jen's little verbal jab and let it pass. Jen was perfect in every way. Even her parents called her Perfect Jen.

"Backwards Bob and I were just wondering if you were going to learn how to fly before the end of next summer?" asked Perfect Jen.

".eihtuR olleH (Hello Ruthie)," said Backwards Bob, a yellow-billed mallard who can fly and walk frontwards but can only speak backwards.

"Hello Bob," Ruthie said to Backwards Bob.

Backwards Bob understood frontwards talk; he just could not speak frontwards. Backwards Bob didn't speak much. As a result, Perfect Jen liked to hang around with Backwards Bob. With Backwards Bob around, she could do all the talking while Backwards Bob did all the listening. Backwards Bob would stand there, listening to Perfect Jen for what seemed like hours, and just say ".neJ seY" (Yes Jen) until she finally stopped talking. This was just ideal for Perfect Jen because there was nothing she liked more than to hear herself speak.

Ruthie was in no mood to argue with Perfect Jen that night. She was tired from all her practicing. She was tired of worrying if she was going to ever learn to fly. She was tired of all the ribbing from her friends. She just wanted to enjoy her first fireworks show. She just ignored Perfect Jen and turned back towards KT and The Answer.

Flying would have to wait until another day, fireworks were much more important or at least that's what she thought.

"Come on guys. It's beginning to get dark. I bet the show is going to start soon. All the humans are mingling and sitting down, and it looks like something is going to happen real soon," Ruthie said to her friends.

The group made their way over towards the far edge of the wall to get a better view of the show. Humans and birds, of all shapes and sizes, were filing into Central Park as the big clock from the bell tower rang out nine bells.

"I am sooooo excited," Ruthie said aloud.

".oot eM" (Me too)," said Backwards Bob.

"Me too," said The Answer.

"Me too," said KT.

"Me too," said Evan, a chubby, little hawk dressed in his favorite Incredible Hawk costume. Evan loved the Incredible Hawk so much he usually talked in his best Incredible Hawk voice.

"Yeah, me too," said Perfect Jen.

Not paying attention to what was going on behind them the group stared off into the night sky scanning for any signs of activity. At that very moment, a fat human in a small hat set off a single firework from the field directly behind the group of friends. The firework lifted off the ground and quickly headed in the group's direction. They had no idea it was heading their way. As each second passed the firework got closer and closer!

"! tuo hctaW" (Watch out!)," cried Backwards Bob. It was too late; the firework exploded a foot or so behind the group.

Backwards Bob, who saw the firework coming, dove to his right, Perfect Jen and The Answer followed him. Backwards Bob fell on Perfect Jen who fell on The Answer making a Perfect Jen sandwich. The Answer and Backwards Bob were the bread and Perfect Jen was the filling. KT fell forward tripping over The Answer's out stretched foot before catching her balance.

And Ruthie B. Goose…Ruthie B. Goose nearly jumped right out of her feathers. She leaped in the air, flapped her wings as hard as she could and that little girl took off in flight!!!

"Ruthie! You're flying! You're really flying!" cried KT.

"Well, what do you know Penguin? You are flying," cried Perfect Jen in disbelief.

"You did it. You did it. You finally did it," said The Answer.

"Up and away you go!" Evan said in his Incredible Hawk voice.

"ylF!!! ylF!!! lrig oG (Fly! Fly! Go girl!)," said Backwards Bob from the bottom of the Perfect Jen sandwich.

"Well, what do you know? I am flying," Ruthie said to herself as she rose a few feet off the ground. "I knew I could," she called out to her friends calmly. Inside she could hardly contain her excitement.

The fireworks show came and went. Ruthie "oohed" and "ahhhed" with her friends during the entire show, in truth all she could remember was the fantastic feeling she got when she finally flew for the first time.

I came to pick her up, right at ten o'clock. She gave KT a hug, said good night to her friends then jumped up on my back. She didn't say a word. Off we went.

"How was the show dear?" I asked as we approached our home.

"Great Daddy," she said. "It all started with a big bang."

CHAPTER 4
The Incredible Hawk

Ruthie decided to keep her first solo flight a secret. She chose not to tell us for one more day. She told us later that she had a plan but wasn't sure how to launch it until the Incredible Hawk showed her the way.

It was Friday. It was close to 7 p.m. and that meant our house was going to be jammed with kids. You see Friday night at 7 p.m. is The Incredible Hawk time at our house. Every Friday from 7 p.m. to 8 p.m. on Channel 21, the Chickalodeon channel, the *High Flying Adventures of the Incredible Hawk,* is shown.

For the last two years, the Incredible Hawk has fought crime and injustice from his secret lair high atop the Empire State Building in New York City. He quickly has become the most popular superhero for young birds and their parents everywhere. Little birds truly admire him. No bird would ever think of missing an adventure of the Incredible Hawk. My little Ruthie B. is one of his biggest fans.

"Hurry, Mommy. The guys will be here soon. Are the snacks ready? Make sure you put lots of butter on the popcorn (knowing full well that Perfect Jen HATED butter on her popcorn)," Ruthie said.

"Please go and answer the door Ruthie," I said. "I think your guests are here."

Ruthie quickly went to answer the door. KT and The Answer strolled in and took their usual spots in front of the TV.

"Hey Mr. B.," chimed the pair.

"I've got one for you Marty…I mean The Answer," I said.

"Here's a tricky one for you. How many inches are there in a mile?" I asked.

"That's an easy one Mr. B. Everyone knows that there are 5,280 feet in a mile and of course, 12 inches makes one foot so naturally there are 63,360 inches in a mile," said The Answer

"You did it again Marty," I said. "You are indeed The Answer."

"Greetings and salutations good citizens, are you ready for another fine adventure?" Ruthie's friend Evan said, entering the room wearing his favorite Incredible Hawk costume, in his Incredible Hawk voice.

Moments later Backwards Bob arrived with Perfect Jen directly behind him. The gang was all here.

"ydobyrevE yeH (Hey Everybody)," said Backwards Bob.

"Hey!" they all screamed.

Everyone screamed except my wife. Even after being around him for the last few months she still could not understand what Backwards Bob was saying and it just drove her crazy.

"What'd he say?" my wife quietly asked me. "I can never understand what that boy is saying."

I just smiled at her and shook my head in disbelief. It was fun to have all the kids in the house.

The snacks were in place and the kids were in their favorite spots. Ruthie and KT were sitting on the floor inches from the screen. The Answer was perched as far back from the TV as he could be in the corner of the room. Perfect Jen was situated a perfect four and one half feet and slightly to the right of the TV (the perfect place to watch TV according to some article she read.) Backwards Bob was squatting just to the left of her and two steps back. The Mrs. and I were in the back, sitting on the couch. The TV was tuned to Channel 21 just as the clock struck seven. Ruthie could hardly contain herself. Even though she had seen every episode for the last two years she still treated it like it was her first time.

"Greetings and salutations good citizens, are you ready for another fine adventure? The Incredible Hawk welcomes you. Let the adventure begin!" screamed the Incredible Hawk from the TV set.

"Hey!!! Who put the butter on the popcorn? You know I don't like butter!" exclaimed Perfect Jen.

"Hush…I am missing the show," said Ruthie with a smirk.

"Yeah Jen, it's just starting to get good. Incredible is going to take down both those bad guys with one punch!" said Evan.

The show continued while the kids cheered on their favorite superhero as he worked his way past a group of villains, in yet another stirring victory over the forces of evil.

"Up and away!!!" cried the Incredible Hawk from the TV set as he soared off into the night sky. "Up and away!!! Yet another victory for justice, another victory for the Incredible Hawk."

The gang all applauded and screamed their approval. It really WAS a good episode!

"What a great show," said Ruthie knowing how truly great it was. She finally had her plan and now knew how to launch it.

"I just love the Incredible Hawk. He's just the best," said KT.

"tseb ehT (The best)," said Backwards Bob. "tseb ehT"

"Up and Away!" said Evan in his Incredible Hawk voice. "The Incredible Hawk must go."

"I'm with you Evan. I told my mom I'd be home by eight-thirty," said The Answer.

"I'll think of one to stump you next time Marty," I said as The Answer made his way out the front door.

"See you Penguin. I have to go as well," said Perfect Jen. "Are you coming Bob?"

"neJ seY" (Yes Jen)," said Backwards Bob following Perfect Jen out the door.

"I can hang for a little while Ruthie if you'd like to do something," said KT.

"Great, let's go to my room. There's something I NEED to tell you," said Ruthie in a very serious tone.

The two girls walked into Ruthie's room and Ruthie closed her bedroom door behind them. All I could hear was Ruthie saying "The Incredible Hawk is the best."

Something was up, only I'd have to wait until morning to find out exactly what.

CHAPTER 5
The Plan

The moment she first lifted off the ground by herself on that July 4th night, Ruthie realized what she was born to do. She wanted to tell everyone she could fly but she also knew she wanted to keep her flying a secret from her family and friends until she had a plan. Ruthie needed to come up with a plan on how to accomplish her life's goal. Tonight thanks to the Incredible Hawk, The Plan, her plan, finally came to her. She needed to share her plan with her best friend KT before she burst. She was very excited. She had her plan. She had to tell her best friend. Only after she shared her plan with KT would she let the cat out of the bag and tell her family and the rest of her friends of her dream.

"Sit down," she said to KT "I've got it."

"You've got what?" asked KT.

"I know how I'm going to do it," Ruthie said.

"Do what? What are you talking about?" asked KT.

"I know how I'm going to fly higher than any bird has ever flown, I'm going to break the world record," Ruthie said.

"You are going to do what? Fly higher than any bird? Break the world record? You've been watching too many Incredible Hawk adventures. You just started flying a few days ago and now you are going to fly higher than any bird has ever flown and break some world record?" asked KT.

"Yes. That's what I was born to do. I know it! Since the other night at the fireworks, when I first lifted off by myself, I just knew it. Tonight, while we were watching the Incredible Hawk, it all fell into place," Ruthie said.

"You are crazy. Lifted off by all by yourself? Silly goose, a firework scared you! You nearly jumped out of your feathers. You flew exactly two feet off the ground. And now you want to break the world record and fly higher than any bird has ever flown. Exactly how high do you have to fly to break this world record?" asked KT.

"I don't know yet," said Ruthie. "I just know that's what I am going to do. Now I have a plan on how I am going to do it."

"You're not like Evan, right? You realize the Incredible Hawk is just a TV show. He's not real. He's just a character on a TV show," said KT.

"Yes, I know," said Ruthie.

"So what's this plan of yours? Have you told your parents yet?" asked KT.

"No, I haven't told anyone. I haven't even told them I can fly on my own. I think I'll tell them in the morning but I have to tell someone before I explode. You're my best friend; I wanted to tell you first. I need you to believe in me because a lot of birds are not going to. I am going to need your help to break the record," said Ruthie.

"Me? You wanted to tell me first? Wow!" said KT as she reached over to give Ruthie a big hug."I believe in you. I always have and always will. You know you're my best friend too? Now, what's your big plan? Tell me, tell me all of it."

Ruthie hugged KT back and began sharing her plan with her friend right there in the middle of her bedroom floor. She could hardly believe how well it played out, how easily it flowed from her mouth and how much sense it all made. KT appeared quite impressed. She was nodding a lot, while Ruthie was speaking and didn't ask too many questions. A plan this big must have needed time for someone to digest it.

That night after KT left, Ruthie thought about telling us she could fly and about her plan, but decided to wait until morning. For one more night The Plan would be just hers (and now KT's as well).

CHAPTER 6
Step 1

The next morning Ruthie dropped the bomb on us. She told us about the fireworks and her first lift off, her revelation that she was born to fly and her dream to fly higher than any bird has ever flown. She told us she was born to break the world record. She told us she had a plan and she asked us to trust her. World record? Just what was this plan? She told us she'd tell us her plan in due time, but for now she asked that we trust her. Trusting her was easier said than done. It was a lot to throw at a mom and dad before breakfast.

Her mom and I while both very proud of her, were extremely puzzled by Ruthie's announcement. We were proud of her for learning to fly on her own. We knew how much work she had put in and we were thrilled to see her accomplish her goal. We were puzzled and concerned with her new "high flying" goal and this world record. Here was our little girl who had just learned how to fly a few days ago, wanting to fly to record breaking heights. She said she had a plan, but what was the plan? For now I guess we just had to trust her, and that wasn't going to be easy.

That afternoon, Ruthie met up with the gang at their usual meeting spot, the wall below our tree. Ruthie flew there by herself. This was the first time we had seen her fly on her own. Mom and I watched her, through our window, take off from our branch and manage her way down to the wall. She did rather well! She made a landing Perfect Jen would have been jealous of! We were both very excited for her. She descended sixty seven feet all by herself. We were both nervous as new kittens. I wasn't sure if either of us could take watching her make the same flight home, a sixty seven foot ascent. It all seemed a bit scarier for us than it was for her!

The gang was all there, everyone except Perfect Jen and Backwards Bob. Perfect Jen was late for everything, being on-time was the one thing she wasn't quite perfect at yet. Ruthie decided to wait a few more moments for the pair to fly in. Telling the gang her plan wouldn't be as much fun if Perfect Jen wasn't there.

Backwards Bob soon swooped in and Perfect Jen followed making a perfect landing right behind him.

"The gang's all here," said KT. "Go ahead Ruthie, tell them."

"Tell us what? What's up Penguin? You asked us all here for some big announcement, well we are all here. What's the big news?" Perfect Jen snapped back in a sharp tone.

Ruthie then began to tell the gang about her dream of breaking the world record. She told them that she was going to fly higher than any bird has ever flown. They all listened, each in their own unique way, to her story. Ruthie began to recount her first night of flight, her realization that she was born to break the world record and finally how she came up with a plan to accomplish this goal while watching the Incredible Hawk on *Chickalodean.*

"I have a plan, The Plan. This IS going to happen," she said.

They didn't seem too convinced. They all had their own doubts, all except her best friend, KT.

"Marty, I mean The Answer, how high is the highest tree at the highest point in Central Park?" asked Ruthie.

"That would be at Summit Rock; the Old Yellow Poplar, of course. The Rock is 137 1/2 feet high and Old Yellow is 348 ft tall. That's pretty high you know. A lot of the older kids hang out there. Even if you could fly that high, you'd need someone to fly up there with you, just in case there might be any trouble," said The Answer.

"That's where we begin, Step 1 of The Plan. On Wednesday I am going to fly to the top of Old Yellow. Who's coming with me?" Ruthie asked.

"I'm in!" cried The Answer.

"You know I'll be there," exclaimed KT.

"For the protection of all that is good, the Incredible Hawk is always there," said Evan. "I'll be there."

"ni em tnuoC" (Count me in), said Backwards Bob.

"I've got to see this. There's no way you're going to make it halfway up Old Yellow, Penguin," added Perfect Jen. "I want to be there to see it myself. I wouldn't miss it for a million dollars."

"You'll see. I have a plan and this is just Step 1," said Ruthie.

CHAPTER 7
Sully and Ruthie's Tree

Ruthie spent the next few days flying.

She flew around our tree in circles, sometimes twenty five times around without stopping. She flew up to the top. She flew down to the wall. She flew until her wings hurt. She flew on Sunday. She flew on Monday. She flew on Tuesday.

Her mother and I just watched and waited. We needed to find out why she was spending all her time flying to nowhere. We were a bit confused but we trusted her.

On Tuesday Ruthie actually stopped for lunch. That's when I finally had a chance to ask what all the flying was about.

"Little one, you are getting pretty good. I've been watching you. I see you flying round and round. I see you flying up and flying down. You're looking like a real pro. So, what is up? What is this flying all about? What's going on little one?" I asked.

"It's Step 1 Daddy, Step 1 of the plan. Tomorrow I'm going to fly to the top of Old Yellow at Summit Rock on the other side of the park," Ruthie said without blinking an eye.

"Old Yellow at Summit Rock at the corner of the park? That's pretty high isn't it?"

"It's actually quite high, 348 feet high according to Marty. It's the highest tree at the highest point in the entire park. I'm making the flight tomorrow morning. It's Step 1 of The Plan," said Ruthie.

"Well, if The Answer says it 348 feet high then its 348 feet. That boy is never wrong. You think you are ready for something like this? Do you want me and mom to go with you?" I asked.

"No, you guys don't have to come; the gang will all be with me, even Perfect Jen. I'm ready. I've been practicing. I'll be fine, trust me, remember?" said Ruthie.

Ruthie went back to her flying after lunch. She flew for four more hours, came in, ate dinner then went right to sleep. She wanted to be certain that she got a good night's rest for Step 1. Old Yellow at Summit Rock awaited her tomorrow.

Ruthie was up early the next day. She watched some TV checking the day's weather on channel 2. The weatherbird and star reporter on NBC (The National Bird Channel), Buzzard Scott, said it was going to be a nice warm day in New York City. Ruthie looked out the window. It was the perfect day for flying, not even a little breeze, just big white puffy clouds in the bright blue sky. It was perfect flying weather. At 9 a.m. Ruthie rose from her favorite TV watching spot and exited our house without saying a word to either of us except "Good bye". Mom and I didn't even have a chance to wish her good luck.

The gang arrived early and were all there waiting at the wall when Ruthie arrived. No one wanted to be late for this, even Perfect Jen was on time. They knew Ruthie wasn't waiting for anyone today and they didn't want to miss this adventure. Step 1 was going to be fun, one way or another.

Ruthie said hello to everyone and outlined her plan for the day. In a few minutes the entire crew lifted off the ground one after the other with Ruthie leading the way.

"Let's fly over to Old Yellow. Stay low and follow me, it's only about fifteen or twenty blocks away," Ruthie said.

They followed her in a straight line, Ruthie, The Answer, Perfect Jen, Backwards Bob and KT. Evan, dressed in his new Incredible Hawk costume, lagged behind.

Ruthie had never actually seen Old Yellow. The Answer flew up next to her as they got close to Summit Rock and pointed over to their left at Old Yellow off in the distance. The group banked left and landed right at the base of Old Yellow.

"Look how high this tree is Ruthie," said KT. "Are you sure you want to do this?"

Just then a group of older birds, tough looking grey pigeons, spotted the group and flew over to see why Ruthie and her friends were hanging around their neighborhood.

"What do we have here? What are you little kids doing so far away from home?" asked a mean looking pigeon.

"My friend Ruthie here is going to fly to the top of Old Yellow today," said The Answer. "We are here to watch her do it."

"You mean this little girl right here? It looks like she just learned how to fly yesterday. There's no way she is flying that high today or any other day. Sully here is the only one of us who I've seen ever make it to the top," said the pigeon. "Hey guys. You've got to see this. This GIRL is going to try to fly to the top of Old Yellow. What do you think Sully? Think she can fly to the top of your tree?"

The group of pigeons had grown as time passed. The initial group of seven or eight grew to twenty two and they were now completely circling around Ruthie and her friends. They all began to tease and mock Ruthie. Sully, the biggest and meanest looking pigeon, was sneering at Ruthie, giving her an evil look and trying to scare her. It wasn't working. Ruthie didn't say one word. She didn't even back down. She just kept looking high in the air up at the top of that big tree.

The ribbing made Ruthie even more certain that she was making the right decision. Step 1 was about to begin. It wasn't going to be Sully's tree for much longer.

"It's time," Ruthie said loud enough for everyone to hear.

"I'll go up with you," said The Answer, the best flyer in her group. "I'll go up with you as high as I can."

"Okay," Ruthie said nodding. "On three we go. 1……………2………………3,"cried Ruthie.

The two took off like rockets, Ruthie first and The Answer right after her. The group of pigeons surrounding them jumped back and watched the pair take off into the summer sky.

"ti od nac uoy eihtuR oG" (Go Ruthie you can do it) yelled Backwards Bob.

"I bet you don't Penguin," said Perfect Jen under her breath though KT and Backwards Bob heard her.

As Ruthie and The Answer climbed higher the noise below got softer and softer. About two thirds of the way up, around 200 feet, they saw the last sign of the other birds. Around 225 feet, The Answer started to fall back. Ruthie kept on going.

"That is it for me," cried The Answer. "It's all you now Ruthie. I know you can do it. Good luck."

Ruthie was now all by herself. Her friends were just small specks on the ground and her parents were at home blocks away. She was up there all by herself. She was doing what she was born to do, she was flying high. Things were going as planned as she reached 300 feet, 48 feet from the top. She was 48 feet from completing Step 1 when a big gust of wind came up from her left and threw her off balance.

"What was that?" she said aloud.

"Buzzard Scott had said there would be no wind," she thought to herself. The big wind had startled her and had thrown her off balance.

"You're not going to make it today, little one, this is my tree," said Sully, the biggest, meanest gray pigeon, from just above her. "This is Sully's tree."

Ruthie began to drop. She fell a few feet hitting her left wing on one of Old Yellow's pointy branches. She began to tumble and hit her right wing on the next pointy branch below. She used all her strength to regain her balance and quickly righted herself. Her wings hurt but she kept flapping them even though she was in pain. She started to rise again. She was going to be okay. Sully looked on in disbelief. He couldn't believe he didn't thwart Ruthie's efforts. Suddenly, Ruthie felt a surge of energy and once again began to climb higher and faster. She was going to make it. She was going to make it to the top of Old Yellow! She could see the top of Old Yellow only a few feet away. Step 1 was just about complete. As she reached the top she grabbed two yellow leaves from the very top branch, the highest point in the park. She took one quick look around in every direction. She saw all of Central Park and her home off in the distance. Flying high was fun!

"This used to be your tree," hollered Ruthie to Sully, "Now it's my tree as well." Ruthie swooped down and dropped one of the big yellow leaves from Old Yellow's top branches right in front of Sully's beak. She carefully clutched a second yellow leaf in her left wing. That one was coming home to Mom and me.

Step 1 was complete.

CHAPTER 8
The Great Ruppell Griffon

Mom and I were very proud of Ruthie for completing Step 1. We were also very happy that she came home in one piece. She didn't say much to us when she got home that day, just, "Step 1 is complete." she then laid a large yellow leaf on the table and went to her room. Knowing the significance of that leaf, my wife quickly got a frame for it, and hung it on the wall above the TV in the living room for everyone to see. That is where it still sits today. Step 1 was a success but what could Step 2 be? Only time would tell. We just had to trust Ruthie, remember?

It was another Friday night close to 7 p.m., Incredible Hawk time. Ruthie's crew began arriving, one by one, a little after 6:30 p.m. By 6:50 p.m. they were all in their usual Incredible Hawk viewing spots. The Answer, Evan, Backwards Bob, Perfect Jen, KT and Ruthie, all began to cheer as the clock struck seven. They were ready watch another adventure and root on their favorite hero.

"Greetings and salutations good citizens, are you ready for another fine adventure? The Incredible Hawk welcomes you. Let the adventure begin!!!!" screamed the Incredible Hawk from the TV set.

The gang happily watched the first half of the show and let out a sigh of disappointment as the episode broke for a commercial.

"Kids, don't move or you'll miss your once in a life time chance to meet a real live legend. Listen and learn how you can meet Ruppell Griffon, right here in New York City, later

this week. This Wednesday from 4 p.m. – 6 p.m. at New York's famous Madison Square Garden in his only tri-state appearance; come and shake the wing of a genuine aviary world record holder. The highest flying bird ever! That's right, world record holder and living legend Ruppell Griffon will be on hand to tell stories of his highest flying adventure and sign copies of his newest book, Ruppell Griffon-A True Hero," said the announcer on TV.

"Hey Penguin, he holds the record that you want to beat," said Perfect Jen. "Maybe you should go see him and tell him you are going to beat his record."

"You should go Ruthie!" said The Answer. "Tell him you're coming after him and his world record."

I could see Ruthie's little brain working right there in front of the television in our living room, and I knew that only meant one thing. I knew what we were going to be doing this Wednesday at 4 p.m.

"Who's Ruppell Griffon?" asked KT.

"Ruppell Griffon is the world record holder for flying higher than any other bird has ever flown," said The Answer "On November 29th, 1975, over the Ivory Coast in West Africa, Ruppell Griffon flew to the record height of 37,900 feet. That's more than a mile and half higher than the summit of Mount Everest, the world's highest mountain."

"That's who you have to beat Ruthie," said KT. "We should go see him. No, we need to go see him."

"Daddy, can we go? I WANT to go see Ruppell Griffon on Wednesday. No, I NEED to go see him on Wednesday," said Ruthie."Pleeeaassssse."

"Yes…we can go," I said, knowing full well she was going to go with or without me.

"I'll go with you," said KT.

"oot og ll'I" (I'll go too), said Backwards Bob.

"What'd he say?" my wife asked only loud enough for me to hear. "I never understand what that kid is saying, never!" she added.

"He said he's going," I said to her with a smile.

"I'm in," said The Answer.

"Count me out," said Perfect Jen. "Who wants to go see some big, boring, ugly, old bird talk about flying? I have better things to do anyway."

"Will the Incredible Hawk be there?" asked Evan in his regular voice.

"No Evan, just Mr. Griffon," KT said with a laugh.

"Then I will stay home," said Evan "Now please quiet down the show is about to come back on."

By now all the kids had lost interest in the show. Evan, in his Incredible Hawk costume, was the only one who was still watching the show as it ended. The rest of the gang's attention was focused on only one thing, seeing Ruppell Griffon. They all marveled at how cool it was going to be to see a real live legend. They were excited by the opportunity to have a brush with greatness and, to be honest; I was a little excited about the chance as well.

CHAPTER 9
The Legends Meet

Wednesday could not come quick enough for Ruthie. She continued to practice her flying, said little about Step 1 and absolutely nothing about her plans for Step 2. She spent little time with her friends, except to talk to them to finalize their plans for Wednesday. She wanted to be certain nothing would mess up her opportunity to meet her new foe face to face. Her main focus for the rest of the week was her meeting with Ruppell Griffon, the enemy.

Wednesday was going to be a very special day. We were all quite excited when it finally arrived. The Mrs. and I decided it was best for the gang to take taxi cabs over to Madison Square Garden. It was quite a few blocks away and we didn't want any of the kids to get lost. There were six of us, so Ruthie, KT and the Mrs. took one cab over (each group perched on to the roof of one of New York City's famous yellow taxis as it made its way downtown to the Garden). The Answer, Backwards Bob and I took a second cab over to the Garden.

Both groups arrived shortly before 4 p.m. and flew up to the
roof of Madison Square Garden. The roof of the large arena
was teaming with birds. Birds of every color, size and
species were there waiting to see the great Griffon. There
was a stage set up in the back right corner of the roof with
an enormous backdrop covered with pictures of Ruppell
Griffon in various poses. The number 37,900 was
emblazoned everywhere. In the center was a large blown up
copy of the cover of his book and his name was in neon lights
across the top of the entire backdrop. This bird WAS a big
deal. On the stage stood a microphone and on the stand was

the name Ruppell from top to bottom in red letters. Hundreds and hundreds of birds stood in front of the stage waiting to hear their hero speak.

We made our way as close to the front of the stage as we could get and decided on a meeting place in case we got separated. The roof was loud and it was hard to hear.

"Quite a crowd," I screamed to my wife as we quickly lost sight of Ruthie and KT.

"Don't get lost. We'll meet at our landing spot when this thing is over," I yelled to the kids.

Ruthie and KT made their way to within three feet of the stage. The Answer and Backwards Bob were right behind them. As the friends settled into their viewing spots an official looking peacock made his way to the microphone.

"Birds and birdettes, parents and kids, thank you for coming today to a truly historic event. Our guest of honor reached heights that no other bird had ever reached before or may ever reach again. He's the world record holder, flying an amazing 37,900 feet high. Please put your wings together and give a warm New York welcome to a true hero to birds everywhere. Please welcome the great Mr. Ruppell Griffon," said the peacock echoing from the microphone.

"Look how huge he is," said KT.

"Yes, he's three feet tall, with a wingspan of over eight feet," said The Answer.

"He doesn't look THAT big," Ruthie said but she was thinking just the opposite. He was pretty big.

Ruppell Giffon was an impressive figure up there on the stage. He was quite a bit older than his pictures but he was still a larger than life presence up there on the stage. In addition to being a real live hero, Griffon was also a great story teller. Having told and retold his story countless times, he had become a master of mesmerizing the crowd. He told the crowd a brief story about growing up in West Africa, his near misses with hunters, his battle with a crazy lion and then gave a long speech about the day he broke the world record, the day he flew to the height of 37,900 ft.

"One day back in '75, I was just out flying. I was quite a bit younger and in great shape, if I may say. It was a very warm day, it's always warm near the Equator, I decided to fly out toward the ocean to cool off," said Griffon to the crowd. "Then it just came to me. I decided to fly UP. I just flew up, rising higher and higher. It kept getting colder and colder. I felt great! Then it started getting windier and windier but I didn't care. I just kept flying higher and higher."

Ruthie was glued to every word. She didn't see or hear a tweet from any of the birds around her. She was focused on every word Ruppell Griffon said. This was the bird she was going to beat. She wanted to know everything about him.

"As I flew higher and higher I looked up and off to my right I saw a big silver and blue jet airplane heading my way. I was probably 1,000 feet below it and maybe 200 feet to the right of it. I knew I could reach it and I thought it would be fun to fly up and touch its wing as it flew by. So that's what I did. I wasn't very smart back then, but I was strong and a fantastic flyer. I flew right up near the wing and gave it a tap. That's when trouble arose. My tail feathers started to get sucked into the engine on the wing of that big old jet plane. It ripped out nearly all of my tail feathers. I thought I was a goner! As I said, I was strong, really strong, way back then and I fought that plane with all my might. I pulled myself from that old engine, righted myself and glided back home. That's how I flew up to 37,900 feet," said Griffon.

He finished telling of his story of glory and paused.

"I bet you are wondering how I knew I flew to 37,900 feet," Griffon said. "With this!" he said as he help up a silver object that had the numbers 37,900 on its face. "This is an altimeter. It tells you how high you are. My father gave it to me when I was a little bird. I happened to have it with me that day. See the numbers, 37,900 feet? Well, those numbers have never changed since that day. When I fought that big old plane and won, I somehow hit the lock button right here and I've never unlocked it or reset it."

The crowd went absolutely crazy with applause. Griffon left the stage with a bow and the official peacock invited the crowd to purchase a copy of Griffon's new book. He told everyone Griffon would be staying and autographing a copy of the book for every bird that bought one that day. No one was going to miss out, NO ONE, he promised.

After the speech Ruthie and her pals quickly made their way to the meeting spot. Ruthie wanted a book, no Ruthie NEEDED a book, and she wanted a chance to meet the great Ruppell Griffon. The four of them found us waiting at our meeting place. Griffon's book was resting gently on my wife's left wing.

"I thought you might want this dear," Mom said. "Daddy said I was crazy but I bought it for you anyway."

"Thanks Mommy. Thanks Daddy," Ruthie said. 'You know I need to wait to see him, don't you?"

"Of course you do," I said. "Sit tight crew. We are going to be here for awhile."

"Mommy, do you have a piece of paper and pencil?" Ruthie asked. "I need to write something."

The Mrs. handed Ruthie a paper and pencil. Ruthie quickly wrote something on the paper, folded it in fours and went to stand in line to meet Ruppell Griffon. KT joined her, while The Answer, Backwards Bob, the Mrs. and I waited and waited and waited.

The two friends joined the line and didn't say more than three words to each other. The line slowly moved forward snaking in and out as each bird got their cherished signature. While Ruthie waited she rehearsed in her mind what she was going to do and what she was going to say to Griffon.

"Next," said the peacock from earlier in the day. "Little girl, you are next. Step up and meet Mr. Griffon."

Ruthie stepped up and looked Ruppell Griffon squarely in the eyes.

"Hello little girl," Griffon said. Griffon was momentarily taken aback by this cute little girl who was staring so intensely at him. He quickly asked, "Would you like me to sign your book?"

Ruthie shook her head no. She didn't say a word to him. She just handed him the piece of folded paper. A flash bulb went off as the local newspaper, the *Daily Bird Call*, took their picture. Griffon paused, unfolded the paper and read it. He looked at Ruthie with a strange gaze. Ruthie just walked off.

"What's your name?" asked the newspaper photographer from *The Daily Bird Call.*

"Her name is Ruthie B. Goose, from Central Park," said KT "Ruthie B. Goose, the next world record holder."

"What did you write on that paper?" asked KT to Ruthie as she hurried to catch up to her friend.

"Nothing," Ruthie said. "I just wrote a number."

"A number?" KT asked. "What number?"

"37,901" said Ruthie. "Just 37,901."

37,901

CHAPTER 10
It Was Just One Picture

After we came home from Ruppell Griffon's speech and book signing Ruthie locked herself in her room with her new book. She read her new book for the rest of the day, coming out only for dinner and to kiss us good night before bed.

The next day, Thursday, we awoke to an extremely loud knock on our front door. It was The Answer and KT. The Answer had a pile of the newspaper, *The Daily Bird Call,* in his wings stacked all the way up past his beak. KT was babbling something about being in the paper.

"Where's Ruthie?" KT gasped trying to catch her breath. "I need to tell her! I need to tell her!" KT said running towards Ruthie's bedroom.

"She's in her room reading," I said. "She's been reading that book since we got home yesterday."

"Well, we have something else for her to read," said The Answer. "I know she's going to be interested in this."

The Answer handed my wife and I a copies of the newspaper and told us to look at the bottom of the front page.

Right there on the front page was a picture of our little Ruthie with Ruppell Griffon standing next to her holding a piece of paper. The headline above the photo read "**Central Park Girl Challenges High Flying Hero**."

KT quickly disappeared into Ruthie's room to brief her on the newspaper article.

The article read, "*…while the great Ruppell Griffon made an impression on thousands of fans yesterday, during his Madison Square Garden appearance, one fan made a very special impression on him.*

"This cute little girl handed me a piece of paper with the number 37,901 on it, which of course is one foot greater than my world record flight," said the Great Griffon. "As she was leaving, her little friend told us her name and claimed her friend was going to break my world record. I'm going to have to watch out for her. This little girl's name is Ruthie B. Goose of Central Park."

"How wonderful honey," my wife said to Ruthie as she entered the kitchen with KT. "We are going to have to frame this and put it right up there on the wall with your yellow leaf."

Ruthie was not too happy with the sudden publicity. If KT had not said something at the Griffon event, no one would have known about her dream. Now the whole bird world would know, and there wasn't anything she could do about it. She wasn't a happy bird at all.

"This is great," The Answer said, "you're going to be an instant celebrity. Can I have your autograph little girl?" he said jokingly.

The thought of all the attention made Ruthie even madder and I could see she was about ready to blow.

"Look at all the publicity," KT said. "Isn't it great?"

"Great??? Great??? It's the worst thing that has ever happened to me and it's entirely your fault. If you didn't open your big beak yesterday this never would have happened!"

"It was just one picture. I was oooonnnly trying to hhhelp," said KT fighting back her tears.

"You helped alright," said Ruthie in a huff as she stormed back toward her bedroom. "You helped alright!"

KT began to cry. She walked toward our front door to leave until my wife grabbed her. She was heart-broken.

"Hold on honey," my wife said as she comforted KT, "you are not going anywhere."

I quickly walked into Ruthie's room and scolded her for her behavior.

"That's no way to behave and no way to speak to your best friend," I said to her.

"You're right Daddy," she said. "I'm sorry. I was just mad about what happened."

"Don't tell me you are sorry," I said. "Tell KT. She's out in the living room upset and crying."

Ruthie ran out, grabbed KT and said her apologies. The two friends embraced. They were best friends again. Everything was back to normal. Crisis averted.

"Come on. I will never be upset with you again. I promise," said Ruthie. "You are my best friend. Let's go to my room. I've got something to tell you."

KT smiled and followed Ruthie to her room. Ruthie closed the door.

"I'm ready," Ruthie said to KT as the girls found comfortable places on the floor in the middle of the room.

"Ready for what?" asked KT.

"Step 2," Ruthie said.

"Step 2!" KT said excitedly.

"Yes, Step 2 and you are the first to know. I'll tell everyone else tomorrow night after the Incredible Hawk," said Ruthie.

Ruthie then shared her plan for Step 2 with KT. KT loved it!

"Step 2 will be a big hit," said KT.

"Well at least I know Evan will like it," said Ruthie.

CHAPTER 11
Step 2 & The Incredible Hawk's Secret Lair

Ruthie and KT came out of her room, embraced once again and said their goodbyes. Ruthie spent the rest of the day and most of the next day practicing her flying. Every now and then I'd look out to check on her. She seemed to be doing just fine. It looked like she was practicing a lot of climbing and nose diving but I wasn't sure why. She was however getting pretty good.

It was Friday night and we were sitting down for dinner before the crew came over to watch the Incredible Hawk.

"I was watching you today," I said to Ruthie. "You are getting pretty good."

"Thanks Daddy," Ruthie said "I've got to practice a lot in the next few days because Step 2 will happen on Wednesday."

"Step 2 is this Wednesday?" asked my wife. "You just finished Step 1. Don't you think you are moving too fast?"

"Step 2 already? Little one, I think you should slow down a bit. This is all happening so fast," I said.

"Don't worry Mommy and Daddy, I've been practicing. I'm ready for Step 2. Trust me, remember?" Ruthie said.

"Trust you?" I said. "We trust you. But this is happening so fast. What is Step 2 anyway?"

"Well Step 2 is…" she said pausing, "I'll tell you after the Incredible Hawk tonight."

The Mrs. and I pressed her to see if we could coax Step 2 from her but Ruthie wasn't blabbing.

After dinner and clean up, we prepared for the invasion. The Mrs. got the snacks ready, I made sure the living room was clean and Ruthie called all her friends to make sure they were all coming over.

The gang arrived, one by one, exchanged greetings and settled into their normal spots. They were all present, The Answer, Perfect Jen, Backwards Bob, Evan and KT. I decided to try to finally stump The Answer.

"Marty, I mean The Answer, I have one for you," I said.

"Lay it on me Mr. B." said The Answer. "You know you still haven't been able to stump me."

"Okay kiddo, here's one that I know will be a toughie. What can run but never walks, has a mouth but never talks, has a head but never weeps, and has a bed but never sleeps?" I asked.

"Ooh...a tricky one," The Answer said, "What can run but never walks, has a mouth but never talks, has a head but never weeps, and has a bed but never sleeps???...."

"No stalling...Guys, I think I've finally gotten him," I said.

"Oh, no you don't, I don't think so, not with an easy one like this," The Answer said. "The answer is...a river."

"Oh...I can't believe you got that one so quickly. You are right again. I guess that's why they call you The Answer," I said.

Everyone in the room laughed.

The show was just about to start. The room grew quiet as the Incredible Hawk filled the TV screen.

In this week's adventure, the Incredible Hawk saved a poor robin and her chicks from being thrown out of their home by an evil crow banker. It was not one of his best episodes, in my humble opinion, but the kids didn't care. They really loved it.

As the show came to a close, Ruthie stood up.

"I am ready for Step 2," she said to the room.

"2 petS" (Step 2) said Backwards Bob. "ti si tahW (What is it?)"

"Penguin, you did so well in Step 1 and now you're in the newspapers and all, we just can't wait to find out what Step 2 is," said Perfect Jen sarcastically.

"Yes dear, please tell us," said my wife.

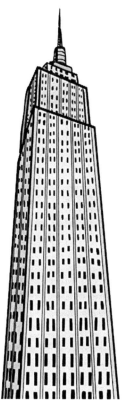

"Okay…Okay…Well I've made it to the top of the highest point in the park. On Wednesday, I am going to fly to the highest place in New York City," Ruthie said.

"You are going to fly to the top of the Empire State Building?" The Answer said jumping up and down. "You're going to fly to the top of the Empire State Building?"

"To my secret lair," said Evan in his Incredible Hawk voice, "high atop the Empire State Building!"

"Yes Evan, that is where I'm going," Ruthie said. "I am going to see the Incredible Hawk in his secret lair, high atop the Empire State Building. That is Step 2 and I'm going to the top of the Empire State Builder this Wednesday at 12 noon."

CHAPTER 12
102 Stories

T he next morning, Saturday morning, Ruthie said little to us about Step 2. She ate breakfast, her usual corn muffin, and flew down to the wall behind our tree to meet her friends.

When Ruthie arrived at the wall everyone was there except for Perfect Jen. The gang was discussing Ruthie's announcement and were eager to help her in any way they could.

"You know the Empire State Building is New York City's tallest building. It is 1,453 feet, 8 -9/16th inches to top of its lightning rod and has 102 stories," said The Answer.

"That's a lot of stories," said Evan in his real voice, "Can you tell me some of them?" he asked.

The gang giggled.

"No Evan. Stories…as in the number of floors it has…the building has 102 floors," said KT.

"The building also has 73 elevators," said The Answer. "Did you know it is possible to ride from the lobby to the 86th floor in less than one minute? I'll bet it is going to take you a little longer than a minute to get that high Ruthie," he said.

"eihtuR ? (Ruthie)" asked Backwards Bob.

"Yes Bob," answered Ruthie.

"ti od uoy naC? (Can you do it?)," asked Backwards Bob.

"She can do it!" answered KT. "I know she can do it and I bet she'll have 102 stories to tell about it!"

CHAPTER 13
Alert the Press

"Good morning and happy Monday to you," chirped a pleasant sounding voice on the other end of the phone. "Thank you for calling the *Daily Bird Call*. How may I direct your call?"

"News Desk please," she said.

"Hello, News Desk," said a quick talking parrot at the other end of the line. "Talk to me. Time is money. What do you have for me?"

"I've got a tip for you," she said. "Are you interested?"

"If it is good I am," said the parrot. "What's it going to cost me?"

"Nothing, it is free, it's not going to cost you anything," she said.

"I like free," said the parrot grabbing his note pad and a pencil from his desk. "Okay, shoot. I'm ready for you. Whatcha got?"

"You know that little bird from Central Park, the one who said she was going to break Ruppell Griffon's world record?" she asked.

"Yeah, I know about her. She was in the paper the other day. We've been getting a lot of e-mails and calls about her since we ran that picture and story. Great bird-interest story don't you think?" said the parrot.

"Yeah, great....Well, I hear that the little girl is going to try to fly to the top of the Empire State Building on Wednesday at 12 noon. A cute little girl flying to the top of New York City's highest building all by herself, I bet your readers would love to read all about that. It may even sell a few more papers don't you think?" she said.

"That's a good tip honey," said the parrot. "We'll be there. I'd like to see that myself. Oh, by the way honey, what's your name?"

"My name? My name is KT, KT Sparrow from Central Park. I'm one of Ruthie's closest friends. I thought she'd like the publicity," Perfect Jen said quickly hanging up the phone.

"There that'll show her, that big show off. When she fails and doesn't make it in front of all her friends and family that'll show her not to be such a big show off. Then when it hits the papers the next day and everyone sees that she's not really that great...well that's the last we'll hear about Miss Ruthie B. Goose and this stupid record," Perfect Jen said aloud.

Perfect Jen picked up the phone again and began making the same call this time to Buzzard Scott at NBC (the National Bird Channel). She then decided to alert Robin Robinson at *Good Morning Aviarica*.

This was going to be a fun Wednesday after all. Perfect Jen could hardly wait.

Meanwhile back at our tree, Ruthie continued to practice and practice and practice. It was Tuesday night right after dinner. Ruthie was sitting at our dining room table with KT and The Answer, the Mrs. and me. We were all pretty nervous about tomorrow's flight. Step 2, to the top of the Empire State Building, was higher than any of us had ever flown including Ruthie. There was no one available to join Ruthie in her attempt. None of us had ever flown more than eight or ten stories up and Ruthie was planning to fly up 102 stories plus the lightening rod without stopping!

"Ruthie," said The Answer, "I have a friend who might be able to join you on your flight tomorrow. I don't think he'd make it all the way to the top with you but he can fly REALLY high and he's super cool."

Ruthie thought for a minute or so, she had never flown that high and decided it might be nice to have a partner, even if it was only for part of the way.

"The Answer, do you know how fast the wind is up that high?" Ruthie asked.

"The wind speed at the top of the Empire State Building is around 110 miles per hour," The Answer said.

"That's pretty fast dear," I said to her. "It wouldn't hurt to have someone up there with you just in case something happened."

Ruthie was quiet for another minute or so before she spoke. "Okay, your friend can come with me. He can fly as far as he wants, but I'm the only one who gets to fly all the way up to the very top."

The rest of us sighed in relief.

"You have trusted me during this entire quest, so I'm doing this for you so that you won't worry," Ruthie said to us.

Her decision made us all feel a little better. We believed in her but there was no crime in playing it safe.

"Who's your friend?" Ruthie asked. "What's his name?"

"My friend's name is Jake. He's a yellow-billed chough, he kind of looks like a black crow but he's not as big and he's super cool," The Answer said. "I'll call him tonight after I get home. I'll have him meet you at the wall at 9 a.m. tomorrow morning. You guys can meet and fly some before the big flight at noon."

"Great, I'll see you and Jake at 9 a.m. at the wall. KT, you, Evan, Perfect Jen and Backwards Bob can meet up with me and my Mom and Dad here at 11 a.m.," Ruthie said. "KT, please tell everyone not be late. Tomorrow is a big day!"

CHAPTER 14
Say Hello to the Incredible Hawk

Ruthie washed up and got herself ready for bed. It had been a long week and I think Step 2 and all the excitement around it was beginning to take its toll on her. She seemed tired and not quite herself as she prepared to go to sleep.

"Mommy and Daddy....I'm ready for bed. Are you going to tuck me in tonight?" Ruthie called out to us from her bedroom.

"Bed?" I said to my wife. "It's a little bit early for her don't you think?"

"She must want to get a good night's rest for tomorrow," said the Mrs. "She's very excited and determined to succeed."

"We're coming little one," I hollered back.

"We'll be right in dear," said my wife.

We got up from our usual spots on the couch and made our way down the hall towards Ruthie's bedroom. The lights were still on as we entered the room. Ruthie was tucked in her bed cuddled up with her favorite blanket and stuffed worm. She looked more like a little girl than someone who was going to try to break Ruppell Griffon's world record.

"Good night Mommy," Ruthie said as my wife kissed her on the top of her head. "I love you."

"I love you too," my wife said.

"Good night Daddy," Ruthie said. "I love you too."

"Get some rest little one," I said "You have a very big day ahead of you tomorrow."

"Don't worry Daddy, everything will be ok. I'm going to the top of the Empire State Building tomorrow and I'm going to say 'hello' to the Incredible Hawk for Evan," Ruthie said.

"We know you are dear," my wife said as we backed out of Ruthie's room and shut off the lights. We said we loved her, closed the door and left her so she could fall fast asleep.

(Ruthie quickly drifted off to sleep and began to dream)…..

"Hello little girl, what are you doing standing at the bottom of the Empire State Building looking way up towards my perch high above the city?" the bird standing next to her in the street asked.

"You're him….you're the Incredible Hawk," Ruthie said in disbelief.

"I'm going to fly to the top of this building today. I told all my friends I was going to say hello to you when I got up there," Ruthie said.

"Well you can just say 'hello' from right here on the sidewalk, that would be a whole lot easier don't you think?" the Incredible Hawk asked.

"Yes, but how much fun would it be to do that? I like to fly. No, I love to fly and most of all I love to fly very high. Would you like to fly up to the top with me Mr. Hawk? You are the only one I'd let join me," said Ruthie.

"Call me IH," he said "I'm the Incredible Hawk to millions of birds everywhere but you can call me IH. Flying to the top of the Empire State Building with you does sound like a whole lot of fun, but you do realize that it's pretty high up there. Think you can make it?"

"Yes, I know Mr. Hawk...I mean IH. My friend Marty said that it's 1,453 feet to the top but I'm flying to the top today, with or without you. It's Step 2, it's part of my plan. My goal is to soar to 37,901 feet up and break Griffon's world record," Ruthie said.

"That's a big goal for such a small bird, but for some reason I know you're going to break Griffon's record. Some day you're going to break the world record but today we only have to fly to the top of this building," he said. "Are you ready to go?" he asked.

"*I'm ready,*" *said Ruthie.*

"*Then let's goooooooo,*" *he said.* "*Up and away!!!*" *cried the Incredible Hawk as he soared off into the sky.* "*Up and away!!!*"

"*Up and away!!!!*" *cried Ruthie as she soared off into the sky right after the Incredible Hawk* "*Up and away!!!*"

Ruthie took aim at the Incredible Hawk's tail feathers and began her chase upwards. She kept flying higher and higher chasing the Incredible Hawk. She kept pushing herself harder and faster, higher and higher but she just couldn't catch him. "*Slow down*", *she thought to herself but then decided she needed to fly even faster if she was going to catch up with her hero.*

In an instance, she looked down to see how high she was and then quickly looked back up. She lost him. She had lost sight of the Incredible Hawk. Where did he go? She was two-thirds of the way up, alone and had no idea where her hero and co-flyer was.

Ruthie kept pushing on. She kept flying even higher and higher but still there was no sign of the Incredible Hawk anywhere. She was now flying even faster, really, really fast, faster than she had ever flown in her life and she was having fun. Looking up, she could see the tip top of the building, the lightening rod and off in the distance she could see the Incredible Hawk. He was standing at the top corner of the building waiting for her. He was right there waving his right wing.

"*Hello Ruthie B. I've been waiting for you,*" *he screamed.*

"Hello IH," said Ruthie as she zipped passed him. I told Evan I would say "Hello" to the Incredible Hawk when I reached the top. So here I am, "Hello Incredible Hawk!"

Ruthie opened her eyes and sat up. "Was it a dream?"she asked herself. It was so real, but it was all just a dream. She just smiled and laughed.

I heard commotion coming from her room and opened the door to Ruthie's bedroom to check in on her.

"Is everything okay sweetie?" I asked.

"Yes Daddy, everything is ok, I just had a dream," she said, "but it was a GREAT dream. In my dream I flew to the top of the Empire State Building and said hello to the Incredible Hawk. Tomorrow I'm going to say "hello" to the Incredible Hawk for real. I'll tell you all about it in the morning."

"Sounds like a pretty good dream little one," I said. "Get some rest; you have a big day ahead of you. I love you, good night."

"Good night, Daddy," she said. "I love you too."

With that Ruthie put her head back on her pillow, cuddled her favorite stuffed worm and drifted back to sleep knowing that tomorrow was truly going to be a very BIG day.

CHAPTER 15
A Star Is Born

Ruthie woke up precisely at 7 a.m. My wife and I were already up having breakfast. My wife handed me the newspaper and told me to read an interesting story on the bottom of the front page. As Ruthie came to the table, I quickly put the paper away making certain that she did not see it. I asked her how she slept and mentioned her dream. She said it was the best sleep she'd ever had. She told me all about her Incredible Hawk dream and then grabbed a corn muffin off the table and went into the living room to watch TV to check the day's weather report.

I grabbed the paper and began reading...

"Local Central Park Girl Attempting to Fly to the Top of the Empire State Building Today, the headline read. *Little Ruthie B. Goose, the girl whose goal is to break Ruppell Griffon's world high flying record will be attempting to fly to the very top of New York City's highest building today at 12 noon..."*

I put the paper down.

"Do you think she saw it?" my wife asked.

"No. If she did, we'd know," I said.

"Do you think we should tell her?" asked my wife.

"No, I don't think so. She has enough to worry about with the flight and all. She'll find out soon enough," I said.

"I wonder who spilled the beans. I wonder who told the paper about Ruthie's plan?" my wife asked.

"I'm not sure but I do know one thing, after the other day it wasn't KT," I said.

Ruthie came back into the room with some news. I hid the paper from her making sure she didn't see the article.

"Buzzard Scott on NBC said it was going to be a perfect day for flying," Ruthie said. "No rain in site, not a cloud in the sky. It is going to be a perfect day."

With that Ruthie gave us each a kiss and went whistling out the door to meet The Answer and his friend, Jake.

Once she closed the door, I made a quick call to The Answer hoping to get him before he left.

"Marty?" I said on the phone. "It's Mr. B., Ruthie's dad."

"Yes, Mr. B? Is everything all right? Did you see the article in today's *Daily Bird Call?*" he asked.

"Yes, that's why I'm calling. Ruthie didn't see it, and I don't think it's such a good idea to tell her about it. It's only going to upset her," I said.

"You're right Mr. B. I'll keep a lid on it. I'll tell Jake and the rest of the gang to be tight lipped about it," he said.

"Marty, did you tell the paper about Ruthie's flight?" I asked.

"No I didn't, I wonder who did. I know one thing there is no way KT would say anything," said The Answer. "Mr. B, I've got to get going, Jake is here and we're late. Ruthie doesn't like it when anyone is late."

"I have no idea who spoke to the newspaper either but I'm going to find out. I'll let you guys get going, I'll see you and the gang here at 11 a.m. Good bye," I said. With that I hung up the phone and went back to my breakfast.

Ruthie was at the wall waiting for her friends to arrive. The clock had just stuck nine and the last bell was ringing, The Answer and Jake where nowhere to be found. Ruthie hated when anyone was late and was getting quite restless. Something strange was happening and Ruthie was quite confused. She began to notice that something wasn't quite right. Both friends and strangers were saying hello to her and wishing her good luck. She had realized that she might get a little notoriety from the recent article and picture in the *Daily Bird Call* but it seemed quiet peculiar to her that everyone in the park that morning knew her.

"Good luck little girl," said an owl from his perch near the wall.

"Good luck Ruthie," said Fred the carrier pigeon as he delivered the morning mail.

"Go get'em kid," said Stanley the humming bird, as he flew by.

Weird, she thought. She looked up and saw The Answer and Jake flying in. The duo made a perfect landing next to her on the wall.

"Sorry we are late," The Answer said "This is my good friend Jake."

"Hello," Ruthie said.

"Hi de ho, Kitten," Jake said in a confident swagger.

Jake stood on the wall, chest puffed out with an air of confidence. He was one cool bird. His glossy black feathers and crimson red legs made him look like a TV star. He was quite handsome. His long curved yellow bill made him look like he was constantly sneering, kind of like a young Elvis Presley (*Kids, ask your parents about Elvis*).

"My name is Ruthie, IT IS NOT KITTEN," huffed Ruthie.

"Okay Kitten, calm down, calm down... Ruthie it is then," he said. "Awful boring don't you think? You look like a Kitten to me, but it's your name, you've got to live with it. Kitten, I mean Miss Ruthie of Central Park, are you ready to show me what you've got?"

Ignoring Jake, Ruthie turned her attention to The Answer, maybe he knew what was up.

"Marty, something weird is happening. Birds I don't even know are saying hello to me and wishing me luck," said Ruthie. "Don't you think that's a bit odd?"

"They just probably saw your picture the other day in the paper. It's nothing to worry about," he said. "Why don't you two go have a flight? You only have a couple of hours to practice before we have to leave?"

"You're right," said Ruthie turning in Jake's direction. It was probably nothing. Let's see what this pretty boy has, she thought.

Ruthie decided it was her turn to see if she could ruffle Jake's feathers so she decided to call him Muffin.

"Come on Muffin. It's time to see what YOU'VE GOT," she said.

"Muffin? You must be talking to be me because I'm sooo sweet," said Jake." Okay Kitten, let's go."

With that, Ruthie took off like a rocket. Jake followed. Ruthie was on her home turf. She knew where she was going. She knew her way around every obstacle and was certain she could lose this pretty boy. She began to fly in and out and up and down around trees, past fence posts, around basketball poles and through phone lines. She weaved in and out hoping to lose her new flying partner. Jake was good. He kept up with her through every obstacle. Ruthie decided to fly up. She darted to her left right past the wall and near the field where the man had lit the firework on the Fourth of July. She then went straight up. Jake followed.

Ruthie kept climbing and climbing and climbing and Jake was right there with her. For a moment, she thought maybe she would skip the Empire State Building and go right to Step 4, just keep going for the record right there, but then she just stopped. She leveled off and began to hover like a humming bird high above the field. Jake stopped right there with her. She had a plan. Step 2 was today, and she was sticking with it. The record would come later.

"Nice flying Muffin," Ruthie said to Jake. She turned back towards the ground and made her way back to the wall.

"Nice flying yourself Kitten," said Jake following her every move.

The Answer had seen the entire show from the wall and was impressed with both of them.

"Think my boy Jake can fly with you today?" asked The Answer.

"He's okay," Ruthie said begrudgingly. "I guess he can come if he wants, if he thinks he can keep up with me. What do you think Muffin? Still want to come?"

"You know what Kitten, there's no way you can keep me away," Jake said. "I'll see you in front of the Empire State Building at 12 noon sharp."

"Don't be late! I'm leaving with or without you right at noon," screamed Ruthie to Jake as he flew off. "Don't be late."

Ruthie said thank you and goodbye to The Answer and flew home. She wanted to get some rest before the gang arrived at eleven. She was ready for Step 2.

Ruthie was still napping when the first group of friends began to arrive at 10:45 a.m.

"olleh B .rM (Hello Mr. B), " said Backwards Bob as he entered our home.

"Where's Penguin? Is she ready? She's got a BIG DAY ahead of her, she doesn't want to be late," said Perfect Jen.

"She's still resting. I'll go get her," I said.

I went to get Ruthie, opening her door slowly as to not startle her. She was still sleeping on top of her blankets. Her bed was freshly made but the rest of the room was a mess. No time for cleaning today.

"Little one...little one...it's time to get up. Your friends are starting to arrive," I said to her while rocking her gently.

She opened her eyes and sat up rubbing away the sleep.

"Who's here? What time is it?" she asked.

"Perfect Jen and Backwards Bob are out in the living room," I said. "It's time to get up, it's almost eleven o'clock."

Ruthie walked out of her room and I followed. In the mean time, KT, Evan and The Answer all had arrived. The gang was all here. Ruthie greeted everyone. No one said anything about today's article but I think Perfect Jen may have tried to until the Mrs. stared her down with one of her trademark "oh no you don't girl" looks. We decided to take two cabs over to the Empire State Building. We broke up into almost the same groups as when we headed to the Garden the other day except Perfect Jen and Evan joined my group. Ruthie, KT and the Mrs. took the first cab over (we hopped on the roof of yellow taxis again) and The Answer, Backwards Bob,

Perfect Jen, Evan and I took a second cab over. Perfect Jen was perfectly miserable the entire ride. Marty's friend, Jake, didn't join us. Ruthie told us he was meeting us at the building at noon.

It took quite awhile for us to make our way over to the big building. New York City was teaming with people and birds darting to and fro. It was a very beautiful Wednesday afternoon and everyone was out enjoying the weather. As we approached the building we realized we might have a problem. There was a huge crowd of birds surrounding the Empire State Building. There were birds on every available tree branch, standing on the roof tops of every building surrounding the big building, resting on every fire escape and stationed on every available window sill. It was a pretty impressive crowd of spectators. TV cameras from *NBC* and *ABC* (America Bird Channel) were also there. Buzzard Scott and Robin Robinson were on hand microphones in wing. A reporter, a squawky yellow parrot, and photographer from the *Daily Bird Call* were also present. It was a regular media circus and Ruthie was about to step into the center ring.

"Mommy, what's this all about," Ruthie asked? "How did they find out? Where did they all come from? I just wanted to fly to the top of the building. I just wanted to finish Step 2. They are ruining everything," Ruthie said as their taxicab pulled up to the Empire State Building.

"We didn't want to upset you sweetie," my wife said "but there was a report about today's planned flight in the *Daily Bird Call* this morning. All these birds must have read it in the paper and came down to root you on."

"Don't let it bother you dear," my wife said "Look your father and your friends are already here. They are standing there right in front of the building. You have a job to do. I know you can do it. Don't let this bother you."

Ruthie didn't know what to do. As she left the cab, the crowd of birds erupted in a loud cheer. Flashbulbs went off and the TV cameras mobbed her.

"Are you nervous about today's flight?" asked Buzzard Scott as he pushed his microphone in front of her face.

"How does it feel to have all this attention? How does it feel to be a star?" asked ABC's Robin Robinson.

Ruthie ignored their questions. She glanced up and saw Jake standing at the corner of the building away from the crowd.

"Let's go," she yelled to him.

She flew directly at him, grabbed his right wing and off they went. A few birds tried to follow but she left with such speed that they never had a chance.

"I didn't realize you were such a star, Kitten," said Jake to Ruthie as they made their way past the eighteenth floor.

"I didn't either, until now," she said.

"Well then, I guess today a star is born," he said.

CHAPTER 16
Race You to the Top

KT and Evan, dressed in his brand new Incredible Hawk costume, quickly made their way to the front doors of the Empire State Building. Two giant revolving doors spun as people made their way in and out of the great building. The humans were too busy with their lives to realize that something special was happening in the bird word right above their heads.

"I've got an idea Evan," KT said. "I don't want to miss this. I want to get to the top and see Ruthie make it. There's no way we're going to fly up there, so the only other way up is right there," KT said pointing to the elevators in the lobby of the building.

Evan was not sure he was ready for this adventure.

"Danger ahead," he said to KT in his best Incredible Hawk voice.

"Come on Evan, you know, the Incredible Hawk's secret lair is at the top," KT said. "We can sneak right in. The humans will not even notice us. We are small."

"To my secret lair," said Evan in his Incredible Hawk voice, "high atop the Empire State Building."

"To the very top," said KT leading Evan through the maze of humans and through the revolving door. The two friends then disappeared into the building to meet Ruthie at the top.

Out on the street, our little group had shrunk to five; the Mrs., The Answer, Perfect Jen, Backwards Bob and me. We backed away from the building and found a nice viewing area on the top of a six story building across the street.

"Isn't it nice that all these birds came to see Ruthie," said Perfect Jen. "Look at all the TV reporters, cameras and newspaper photographers. It's great to see all the attention she's getting. I just hope she makes it. If she doesn't, well, it would be real embarrassing. There's not a bird around who won't know about her failure. That would be just terrible."

"Don't worry Perfect Jen, she's going to make it," I said. "By the way, were you the one who alerted the media?"

"Me??? Well...well, I thought it would be nice for Ruthie, you know to give her the credit she deserves. Did I do something wrong?" Perfect Jen asked.

"You know what you did little lady," the Mrs. said to Perfect Jen giving the little cardinal her trademark stare.

"We have more important things to worry about than this dear. We'll deal with it later," I said.

"Do you see them?" asked The Answer looking up at the building. "The wind is coming in from the south, so I bet they are climbing on the west side, our side. If we look up over there I bet we see them."

"meht ees I" (I see them), said Backwards Bob "meht ees I (I see them) ereht revo thgiR (Right over there)," he said pointing to the far back corner of the building.

"There they are," I said pointing in their direction.

I could see the two of them, the sleek black feathers of Jake and the snow-grey feathers of Ruthie against the deep blue summer sky. They appeared to be flying at a nice leisurely pace, almost as if they were just out for a nice Sunday morning fly. They were about thirty stories up and everything looked like it was going well.

Thirty stories up, Ruthie and Jake were having a great time making their way up to the top. Ruthie was leading the way and Jake was flying right with her. At thirty six stories, the wind was not a problem and the warm summer sun made the temperature perfect for both of them. The noise and commotion from the streets below had all but disappeared. It was actually quiet. Most of the humans in the offices in the Empire State Building were off to lunch and the few that remained did not take notice of the two birds that were flying past their windows despite that fact that these birds were flying up.

"How are you holding up, Kitten?" asked Jake.

"I'm doing fine. I didn't think you'd last this long Muffin," Ruthie said.

"I'm right here with you Kitten," he said. "I'll be with you all the way to the top."

"All the way?" she asked.

"All the way Kitten," he said. "Race you to the top!"

CHAPTER 17
Look, It's the Incredible Hawk!

Jake took off with a burst of speed upwards. Until then Ruthie had always led the way. It was her flight and Jake was just supposed to be along for the ride. Ruthie dashed off directly after Jake and quickly caught up to him.

"Hold it there pal," Ruthie said. "This is MY flight!"

"I know Kitten...I know, I was just playing with you," Jake said. "Why do you think I slowed down and let you catch me?"

"Let me catch YOU?" Ruthie asked. "I can catch you any time I want!"

Ruthie increased her speed just a bit and worked her way up just ahead of Jake. They were about halfway up, around fifty stories high, higher than either of them had ever flown. The great building had begun to narrow and it was no longer offering them protection from the increasingly stronger winds.

"Enough playing around Kitten, it's starting to get really windy up here and we're getting pretty high. I told Marty I'd watch out for you. If anything ever happened to you, well, I think he'd never speak to me again," said Jake.

"Okay, okay, agreed," Ruthie said. "No more playing around."

"Let's fly over to the other side of the building and see if the wind is any better over there," Ruthie said.

"You lead the way because I don't want to get you upset with me again and I'll follow," he said.

Ruthie eased her speed, stopped climbing and flew to the other side of the building. Jake followed.

Back on the ground Ruthie's family and friends grew concerned. The two were now small specs against the summer sky but their fans on the ground were able to still see them.

"What's happening?" the Mrs. asked. "Why have they stopped? Where are they going?"

"I'm not sure," I said. "I can't see them any more. They've moved to the other side of the building."

"I bet they are just adjusting because of the wind. Sometimes the wind shifts the higher you go. I bet they are just adjusting because of the wind," said The Answer.

"I hope everything is okay," Perfect Jen with a hint of sarcasism.

"yako si gnihtyrevE," (Everything is okay) said Backwards Bob.

"What did he say?" asked my wife. "Someday I'm going to understand that boy."

"Everything is okay, Mrs. B. Bob said, everything is okay," said The Answer.

"I hope so," said my wife. "I really hope so."

Inside the building it was taking quite a while for KT and Evan to make their way into an elevator to get to the top. They had to dodge humans, cleaning carts and a nasty security guard. They lucked out when they overheard two maintenance men say they needed to get to the roof to check on some faulty wiring. The two friends followed these men, hopped on their maintenance cart and were now hiding in the back of the cart riding up the elevator to the top of the Empire State Building to meet Ruthie.

"Hold on Evan," KT said. "This elevator ride is going to be very fast. Remember, Marty said it only took a minute to get to the top."

"This is fun," Evan said in his regular voice. "I hope we meet the Incredible Hawk up there."

The elevator reached the 102nd floor in less than a minute. The two maintenance men, the only humans on the elevator, got off pushing the cart. KT and Evan jumped off the cart and hid behind a trash barrel next to the elevator in the far corner of the deserted room. The two workers continued pushing their cart towards the Observation Deck door in the opposite corner of the room. The large circular room was empty. All the lights were off and there was no sign of any humans. The sunlight that was shinning in from the windows that encircled the entire room light up most of the room. The elevator door area where the two friends waited patiently was dark. The Observation Deck door had been closed but the men left the door open with their work cart. This is where KT and Evan would go to meet their friend but they had to wait until the coast was clear. The two men who walked out to the Observation Deck could be seen by KT and Evan out on the deck working on something.

Out in the open air seventy stories up, the north side of the building offered better flight conditions for Ruthie and Jake so they decided to stay there. It didn't matter much to Ruthie where she flew from only where she ended up, at the top.

"I like this side much better," said Jake. "You can even see New Jersey from here."

Ruthie hadn't noticed, she was only looking one way and that was up.

"Let's get a bit closer to the building for protection against the wind," she said.

Around the seventy fifth floor, Ruthie's wings were starting to get tired. The wind was beginning to pick up even more. It was stronger and faster than anything she had remembered, 110 miles per hour was what The Answer had said.

"That's it for me Kitten," said Jake. "I'm just about out of gas and I want to be able to help you if something goes wrong. I'm going to rest my wings over on that ledge and watch the rest from here. You win the race, now go and beat the building. You are almost there."

"You go and rest," Ruthie said. "I'm okay. I'm almost there. Step 2 is almost complete."

Ruthie dropped her head and continued on. She figured she had one or two more good bursts of energy in her. She decided to make one more shift to the east side of the building to see if she could beat the wind and find more favorable conditions.

Back on the street, her friends and family continued to look upwards, looking for any sign of movement in the sky.

"I see her," I said. "That's her. I know it."

"Looks like she's approximately seventy five stories up," said The Answer. "Boy, that's really high. She's going to do it Mr. B. She is really going to do it."

"Of course she's going to do it," I said.

I think the happiest bird in our little group was my wife. Perfect Jen on the other hand, was, let's say, not in quite a perfect mood.

On the 102nd floor the maintenance men had gone on a break and KT and Evan had made their way out on to the Observation Deck.

The two friends had jumped up on to the railing and were looking out to see if they could see anything.

"Do you see anything?" Evan asked in his regular voice.

"I think that's her right over there," KT said pointing her wing down and to her left.

"Her?" Evan questioned. "Her? I mean the Incredible Hawk. He's supposed to be up here. He's supposed to be in his secret lair high atop the Empire State Building. Where is he?"

"Evan, he must be out fighting crime," KT said.

"You're right. He must be out on an adventure," Evan said. "I'm going to go out there on the ledge to see if I can see him coming."

"Be careful Evan," KT said. "Please be careful."

With that, Evan inched his way out along the railing to the farthest east corner of the building. KT watched with an uneasy feeling as one of her friends made his way out on the ledge of New York City's tallest building while her other friend attempted to fly to its highest point.

Back in the building, the elevator bell rang and the doors opened. KT hid because she didn't want the workers to see her. To her shock and surprise it wasn't the workers but a photographer from the *Daily Bird Call* and Buzzard Scott with his NBC TV camera.

"Let's set up out there," Scott said to his camera bird pointing to the Observation Deck. "We need to get a shot of this for the six o'clock news."

The three made their way out towards the Observation Deck, cameras in wing ready to capture this amazing flight.

At eighty two stories, Ruthie looked behind her to see if she could see Jake. He was nowhere in sight. She looked back at the building and decided to back off it a bit to see if she could catch sight of the lighting rod at the very top. She was at ninety stories now and fatigue was really setting in. She was very tired and her wings were getting heavy but she continued on. All her training and practicing over the past few weeks were paying off. She thought about what the Incredible Hawk would do and she pressed on.

She looked up and something caught the corner of her eye. What was it? It couldn't be. It just couldn't be him. He's not even real.

"The Incredible Hawk!" she said. "My eyes must be playing tricks on me. I'm getting tired and seeing things. But I think it is him. I think I see the Incredible Hawk. He's right there on the corner of the Empire State Building. He's standing right there on the corner of the building. He's right there waving to me. I can see him but I don't believe it."

Ruthie looked up again, blinked a few times and again she saw what she thought was the Incredible Hawk. He was standing on the corner of the top floor of the building waving his right wing and holding on to the corner of the building with his left. He was waving to her and she was flying right to him.

Up she went....93 stories, 94 stories, 95 stories, 96 stories, 97 stories, 98 stories.

"Come on Ruthie, you can do it!!" The Incredible Hawk yelled. "The Incredible Hawk knows you can."

Can it be? Can he be real? Wait until Evan hears this. Ruthie kept pressing on flapping her wings even harder and harder. Almost there, almost to the top and the Incredible Hawk IS real! He is right there a few stories above her. He is real. Can't wait to tell Evan and the gang, she thought.

99 stories, 100 stories, 101 stories...

Evan? Wait a minute, that's not the Incredible Hawk....that's Evan in his Incredible Hawk costume and look there's KT. Look there's Buzzard Scott and the guy from the *Daily Bird Call*. Ruthie waved to each of them as she passed by yelling "Thank you!!!"

102 stories!!!

Down on the ground, her friends and family chirped for joy. They could barely see her that high in the sky but through his binoculars The Answer could see that she had made it to 102 stories and passed on the information.

"ti did ehS (She did it) ti did ehS (She did it)," said Backwards Bob.

"Not yet," The Answer said. "She may have reached the top floor of the building but she still has to reach the top of the lightening rod to complete Step 2. She needs to make it to the very top!"

Inside back at the top of the building, KT was jumping up and down making sure her friend Ruthie saw her. The photographer was flashing picture after picture hoping to get the perfect shot for the morning edition. Buzzard Scott was beginning to do his TV report making sure he got his shot with Ruthie flying behind him.

Ruthie looked up and set her sights on the top of the lightening rod. She gave her friends another quick wave, flashed the okay sign and flew up towards the top of the lightening rod. She had been thinking about this moment for the last week and had planned in her mind exactly what she was going to do. She kept this part of Step 2 a secret. She had reached the last 250 feet of the flight. She passed the TV and radio antennas as she flew up to the top of the lightening rod. The Empire State Building was hers today if only for a brief moment.

It was eerily quiet up there. She felt a renewed burst of strength despite the fact that the wind was now tossing her left and right.

Only twenty or so more feet to go, now ten, now five...Ruthie reached under her chest feathers and found the special small red flag she had tucked there before she left home. She quickly unfurled it, revealing a grey feather sitting on a bright red background with the words STEP 2 in yellow letters sewn in above the feathers on the flag. She came to rest on the very top of the lightening rod. Ruthie carefully tied the flag to the end of the rod making sure it stayed in place. Ruthie gave one quick look in all directions, noticed the great view and took off. She looked back with pride as she saw her newly placed red flag dancing in the breeze for everyone to see. Step 2 was officially complete!

CHAPTER 18
A Gift from The Legend

Ruthie was tired, her wings hurt and she was spent. She thought about joining Evan and KT on the Observation Deck but decided that taking the elevator down was cheating. Besides, she really didn't want to speak with Buzzard Scott and had no desire to be in the *Daily Bird Call* again. She coasted down past her two friends, gave them a quick wave and yelled that she'd meet them down on the ground.

Ruthie continued to glide down taking a leisurely circular path around the building. She kept looking for Jake but he was nowhere to be found. She was disappointed because she was starting to really like Jake in the short time they had spent together. She was looking forward to telling him about the last leg of her flight. They'd have to meet up on the ground later so she could fill him in.

On the ground, all the birds were chirping for Ruthie and flapping their wings in approval. Her family and friends had made their way down off the building where they had been watching Ruthie's flight and were waiting on the sidewalk at the front of the great building for her to return.

"Here she comes," said the Mrs. pointing toward the sky.

"reh ees I (I see her)," exclaimed Backwards Bob.

"Yeah, here she comes," proclaimed Perfect Jen in a perfectly unhappy tone.

"I wonder what Step 3 is?" commented The Answer.

"What did I hear? Well, I guess there IS something The Answer doesn't know," I said. "We just finished Step 2. Let's let Step 3 come another day."

Just then, KT and Evan came running out of the building with the media trio directly behind them.

"Is she down yet?" asked Buzzard Scott.

"No not yet," said Perfect Jen "but she'll be here soon enough."

KT and Evan joined us as we waited for Ruthie to finish her final ten stories down. As Ruthie planted her two feet on the ground landing gently on the sidewalk directly in front of us, the crowd of birds erupted in one last cheer. The newspaper photographer snapped one last picture and Buzzard Scott wrapped up his newscast with one last comment. Ruthie gave each of us a big hug and kiss and said, "See I told you to trust me." And trust her we did.

Our group all flew home to Central Park. Ruthie jumped on my back like she used to do before she learned to fly and fell asleep half way home. All of her family and friends were so proud of her and glad Step 2 was finally over. The Mrs. was the happiest of all. I think that even Perfect Jen was happy for Ruthie in her own unique way.

When we arrived home I put Ruthie right to bed. The Mrs. and I made sure we didn't miss any of the evening news reports. Robin Robinson's report was short and sweet, it was okay. Buzzard Scott's report was by far the best. He had all sorts of shots of Ruthie and even showed one with the Mrs. and me.

I woke up early the next morning and went out and got extra copies of the *Daily Bird Call*. There were three stories about Ruthie on the front page and an entire page of pictures on page three. The Mrs. quickly cut out each of the articles, framed them and placed them on the living room wall with Ruthie's other mementos. Ruthie finally awoke at around 11:15 a.m. that morning. She didn't even look at the newspapers despite that fact they were sitting all over the breakfast table. She didn't even say a word to either of us about her flight. She said good morning and grabbed her usual corn muffin. She did however have an ear-to-ear grin that appeared as if it may never fade away.

Ruthie was sitting at the table finishing her muffin when there was a knock at the door.

"I'll get it," Ruthie said jumping off her seat. "I bet it's KT. I asked her to come over around noon so we could play."

Ruthie walked to the front door to greet her guest while the Mrs. and I remained at the breakfast table.

"It's you….It's you," Ruth said stuttering a bit as she said it.

"WWWhat are you doing here?" she asked.

"Is that any way to greet an aged legend?" asked the deep voice. "Aren't you going to ask me to come in?"

"Yes. Come in. Please come in," Ruthie said.

In the door walked this massive creature. He dwarfed Ruthie and made the Mrs. and I feel very tiny. I didn't realize how large a bird he was when I had seen him last week up on stage but here standing in my dining room, Ruppell Griffon seemed like a giant.

"You and I have already met but are you going to introduce me to your parents?" Griffon asked.

"Oh. Sorry, Mom and Dad this is Mr. Ruppell Griffon. Mr. Griffon these are my parents Mr. and Mrs. B. Goose," said Ruthie.

It felt like I was meeting royalty and in many ways I was.

"Welcome to our home Mr. Griffon," I said. "It is truly an honor and a privilege."

"The privilege is all mine sir and madam," said the legend. "Please call me Ruppell."

"Please have a seat," I said. "To what do we owe this honor?"

"I've been keenly following the exploits of your little girl here. I'm very much impressed. She caught my attention at the book signing and since then I've been keeping my eye out for her. That flight to the top of the Empire State Building yesterday was truly a thing of beauty. She's going to break my record some day and I dropped by to give her a little gift that might help her along the way," said Griffon.

"That's extremely kind of you Mr. Griffon," said the Mrs.

"May I have a moment alone with young Ruthie?" Griffon asked as he pulled a small box out from under his huge wing.

"Ruthie, we'll be out in the living room if you need us. Mr. Griffon has something for you," I said.

The Mrs. and I made our way to the living room both wondering what could be inside that box.

"Please come here Ruthie, this is for you," said Griffon as he handed Ruthie the box. "Go ahead, please open it."

Ruthie opened the box and looked inside. It was a small silver device, small enough to clip around a wing or an ankle. It was the same device he held up when he was on stage. It had spinning numbers and the numbers were set to 37,900 (Griffon's record). There was a small round silver button at the top left corner with the words "RESET" on it. Ruthie wasn't quite sure what the device was. She knew it must be special if Griffon came all the way to her house to give it to her in such a nice pretty box.

"It's an altimeter. It tells you how high you are. Actually it's my altimeter. It's THE altimeter I used that day on my record flight. You see, I wasn't just out for a nice flight that November day back in '75. I really wanted to break the world record. Just like you, I wanted to fly higher than any bird had ever flown. Didn't you wonder how I knew how high I was flying on that day? Well that little contraption you are holding in your wing, that's how. It tells you how high you are. See the silver circle, the one on top. Well that resets it back to zero. I have not pressed that button since the day of that flight but today I'm pressing that button. You're going to have to get it back up to 37,900 or higher," said the magnificent bird.

With that Griffon reached over Ruthie's shoulder and pressed the RESET button. The altimeter now read zero

"Now it's really yours," he said. "Go break my record. Get it back to 37,900. If you ever need any advice or help I'll be there for you. I want you to go break my record."

He then handed her a small envelope and said "Please bring this with you on your record flight but keep this a secret between you and me."

Ruthie nodded yes and said thank you.

With that Griffon turned and left our home. Ruthie stood there speechless, wings outstretched, staring at her newest prized possession, the gift from the legend, her priceless new altimeter.

CHAPTER 19
The Incredible Hawk Saves the Day

Ruthie placed her gift and secret envelope in a safe place in her room. For the rest of the day she simply played with KT and Evan. She never mentioned Step 2, Step 3 or Griffon's record. For at least one day any way we had our little girl back.

Friday night was here once again and her friends filed in one by one, the regular group was in attendance except for one new addition, The Answer's friend Jake.

"Mr. B. this is my friend Jake," said The Answer.

"Nice to meet you pops," Jake said to me. "Where's the star? Oh, there you are Kitten," he said to Ruthie as he saw her sitting on the floor in front of the TV waiting for the show to begin.

I had only heard about Jake from The Answer, KT and Ruthie but I never actually had a chance to meet him, until that night. I didn't like him. He was TOO cool for me. I didn't like the way he looked. I didn't like that he called my little girl Kitten. Most of all, I didn't like that he called me pops.

Jake took a spot next to Ruthie on the floor. KT didn't seem too happy about it either. Jake and Ruthie became engrossed in their own conversation so I decide to change the subject.

"Marty, I think I have one that you're not going to get," I said to The Answer. "What happened in 1961 and will not happen again until 6009?"

"Hmmm," The Answer said. "What happened in 1961 and will not happen again until 6009? It's not an eclipse of the sun, it's not a comet and I know it's not the alignment of all the planets...Hmm let me think for a moment......let me think...let me think...oh...very tricky Mr. B...very tricky...this one is one for Backwards Bob isn't it?!"

"I can't believe you got it," I said.

"Got what?" asked Perfect Jen.

"What's the answer?" asked KT.

"It's the next time a year will read the same straight or upside down. Get it? **1961** and **6009**," said the Answer. (*Readers, please hold your book upside down to see what The Answer is talking about*)

"Don't you think that's odd Backwards Bob?" I asked.

"never odd or eveN (Never odd or even),"said Backwards Bob. (*Yes, Readers that's a true palindrome, it's the same forwards as it is backwards*)

"Hey I finally understood him!" screamed my wife.

"Of course you understood him dear. He used a real palindrome, a word or phrase that is the same forwards as it backwards," I said.

"Well that doesn't count now, does it?" asked the Mrs.

"Hey that's pretty cool Backwards Bob," said Evan in his regular voice.

"It should be, he's been saving that one for almost thirteen weeks," said Perfect Jen.

Ruthie and Jake's heads never turned. They continued to have their own little conversation until Evan screamed in his Incredible Hawk voice, "Greetings and salutations good citizens are you ready for another fine adventure?"

The show was about to begin.

"Hey!!! Who put the butter on the popcorn? You know I don't like butter," yelled Perfect Jen.

Ruthie giggled and turned her attention away from Jake and towards the TV.

In this week's show the Incredible Hawk saved an airplane from crashing. He flew up to meet the plane, grabbed it by the tail wing and returned the plane with its passengers home safely. Ruthie never moved, not even an inch, during the entire show. The entire gang cheered hardily when the Incredible Hawk saved the plane even super cool Jake. Ruthie just nodded a lot and remained silent. That meant trouble. She had been thinking of something and found her answer.

After the show Ruthie said good bye to all her friends but asked KT to stay. To the Mrs., KT's and my delight Jake left with The Answer.

"Wait Jake, I'll walk out with you," said Perfect Jen.

Ruthie turned and gave Perfect Jen a nasty look. She turned back away, grabbed KT by the wing and walked to her room.

"The Incredible Hawk saved the day," Ruthie said to KT as they went into her room. "The Incredible Hawk saved the day again."

CHAPTER 20
I've Got to Catch a Plane

Ruthie and KT sat on Ruthie's floor facing each other.

"The Incredible Hawk saved the day once again," Ruthie said.

"Yes I know, I was there remember? I saw the show too," said KT.

"No, you don't understand. Step 3, the Incredible Hawk just gave me the final answer to Step 3," said Ruthie.

"Step 3? You got Step 3 from watching that show?" asked KT.

"Exactly, I have to find out what it's like to be at 30,000 feet but I just couldn't figure out how I was going to do that. I spoke with Griffon about being that high but hearing about it is not the same as actually doing it. Before I can see if I can fly that high, I want to see what it's like to be that high. Tonight, watching the Incredible Hawk I figured it out. I'm going to take a plane. But I'm not going to be on the inside of the plane, I'm going to strap myself to the tail wing of the plane and be on the outside. When it reaches 30,000 feet I will set myself free and then I'll just fly back down to the ground. That's Step 3. Easy, don't you think?" Ruthie said.

"You are going to strap yourself to a plane? Are you coo-coo? That's dangerous. Your parents are never going to let you do it," KT said.

"I know. You are right. Not a word to anyone. Not a word to my mom or my dad. Not a word to Evan, Perfect Jen, Backwards Bob, The Answer. Not a word to the press. Nobody can know. Do you understand? Not a word to anybody!" Ruthie said.

"What about Jake?" KT asked.

"We are going to need his help. There's no way the two of us can get to the airport and strap me to the plane all by ourselves. We are going to need his help," Ruthie said. "But other than the three of us, this is Top SECRET. Do you promise?"

"I promise," KT said nodding her head. She wasn't very happy with the plan and she wasn't too happy that Jake was the only other one involved but she gave her word. She believed in her friend and trusted her. Ruthie's new secret was safe with her.

"When do you plan on doing this?" KT asked.

"On Wednesday, we go for it on Wednesday," said Ruthie. "I'll speak with Jake tomorrow. We'll meet and go over our plan this Sunday."

With that, Ruthie got up from her spot of the floor, opened the door and started to skip towards the kitchen for a late night snack. She forgot all about Perfect Jen for the moment. Everything was great. She was ready for Step 3.

"Come on KT," Ruthie said loud enough for only her to hear. "I've got to catch a plane."

CHAPTER 21
37,901 Feet, the Easy Way

Ruthie woke up early the next day, Saturday and joined us for breakfast. She ate two corn muffins and talked our ear off about everything except the world record or Step 3. She didn't even mention her new friend Jake. Something was up. We just didn't know what.

"I'm going to go out and practice some flying," Ruthie said, "I'll see you after lunch."

She gave each of us a kiss on the beak and strode out the front door. She promptly flew off to the other side of the park.

"That little girl is up to something," the Mrs. said.

"Did you see the way she carried on with THAT BOY Jake last night?" I asked.

"Our little girl is growing up," said the Mrs.

"Yes, I know and I don't like it one bit," I said.

Over on the other side of the park Ruthie flew up to a big branch located near the top of an old hickory tree which was set off by itself in the far corner of the park. She slowly walked to a door at the end of the branch and gave it three quick raps.

Someone's coming, she thought. She stepped back so the bird on the other side could answer the door.

"I'm coming…I'm coming…" said the bird from behind the door. "Who could be knocking on our door so early on a Saturday?" asked the bird from behind the door.

The door slowly opened. It was an older smaller version of Jake. The older bird was all black with a touch of grey all around her face and wings, she was hunched over a bit and she had a red scarf wrapped around her head.

"Yes, may I help you dear?" asked the old bird.

"Yes ma'am, is Jake here?" asked Ruthie.

"Why yes he is darling. Are you a friend of his?" she asked. "Jake, you have another girl here looking for you. Please come to the door. This one's a cute little thing."

All of the sudden Jake came running from inside of the house. His feathers were somewhat rustled and he had a confused look in his eyes.

"Thanks Grandma. It's ok, this is my friend Ruthie," he said. "She's the one I've been telling you about."

"Oh yes. She looks like a nice girl," said Jake's Grandma. "I like her better than the other ones."

"Thanks Grandma," Jake said as he closed the door.

"I'm glad she likes me better than the OTHER ONES," Ruthie said.

"That's just Grandma being Grandma, Kitten," said Jake. "There are no other ones you're my number one Kitten. What brings you here today?"

"Okay, okay…" Ruthie said wondering how many other ones there were, "I came here to tell you about Step 3. We…I need your help again. "

"Anything for you Kitten, I told you that the first day we met. I'm here for you. I like you. You are my friend, whatever you need, I'm here for you. Lay it on me, what can I do to help?"

Ruthie then laid out her entire plan for Step 3. How they were going to get to the airport, how they were going to find a plane and how KT and Jake were going to strap her to the plane so she could reach 30,000 feet the easy way.

Unlike KT, Jake LOVED the plan. He promised to keep it a secret, meet with KT on Sunday to map out the plan and help get Ruthie strapped to the plane on Wednesday.

After going over her plan with Jake one more time, Ruthie was satisfied that everything was in place.

"See you tomorrow on the wall Kitten," Jake said. "I think it's a GREAT plan."

"See you at 2 p.m. and make sure you don't bring the others," Ruthie said.

Ruthie went home and had lunch. She called KT and made arrangement to meet at 2 p.m. at the wall the next day. The rest of the day she spent lounging around watching TV. Something was indeed up, but we still didn't know what.

2 p.m. Sunday afternoon came and KT was already at the wall waiting for Ruthie. Ruthie flew down precisely at 2 p.m.

"Hey KT, where's Jake. I guess he's late. That boy is going to be in trouble, he's not here yet?" Ruthie said.

"Mr. Wonderful has yet to arrive," KT said.

"Mr. Wonderful? Don't you like Jake?" Ruthie asked.

"It's not that I don't like him, it's just that you've been spending a lot of time with him lately. I thought I was your best friend," said KT.

"You are my best friend. You're my BFFL (Best friend for life). He's just my new friend and he's helping me break Griffon's record. You're both helping me break the record," Ruthie said.

"Here he comes," said KT. "He's right over there," she said pointing with her wing outward as Jake flew in for a perfect landing.

"Hello Kitten. Hey KT. Sorry to keep you ladies waiting. I had to finish getting Grandma her lunch," Jake said.

The three sat there on the wall for almost two hours going over the plan. KT continued to state her objections while Ruthie and Jake continued to rebuff her. The three finally agreed on the plan and decided to meet at 9 a.m. on Wednesday morning. Ruthie was catching the 12 noon flight to London and she wasn't going to miss it.

Ruthie spent the next two days practicing her flying. It was way too quiet in our house. None of her friends came to visit. The commotion from the press after the Empire State Building flight had quieted down. Ruthie stopped speaking about Griffon's record or Step 3. We figured something was up.

It was Wednesday and lately something was always happening on Wednesday.

"Today's Wednesday you know," I said to Ruthie.

"Yes Daddy, I know today is Wednesday," Ruthie said wondering if I knew of her plan.

"Lately something always has been happening on Wednesday," I said. "Step 1 was on Wednesday. Step 2 was on Wednesday. Well today is Wednesday, is Step 3 happening today and you just haven't told me yet?"

"Remember what I said when we started this Daddy? Trust me," Ruthie said. "Trust me."

With that, Ruthie gave me a kiss on the cheek and left the house. Trusting her was getting harder and harder with each passing day.

Ruthie picked up KT at her house and the two flew over to Jake's house. Jake was there waiting for them on his branch. As planned the three flew over to LaGuardia Airport which was nine miles to the east in the Queens section of New York City. Once they arrived at the airport, the trio made their way over to Terminal A where there were planes waiting for human passengers to board. There were four white planes and one silver one sitting at the terminal being loaded with human passengers and their luggage.

"That's the one," Ruthie said. "See the silver one right in the middle. That's the G777 set to leave for London right at 12 noon. It's perfect. It is right in the middle of those other planes. The humans will never see us."

Ruthie looked up at the clock at the top of the flight tower. It read 11:37 a.m. They had less than twenty five minutes to fly over to the tail wing, get her strapped in and be ready to go by noon. Ruthie gave it one last mental check before giving the okay for the three of them to make their move.

Fastening rope? Check. Griffon's altimeter? Check. The coast is clear? Check

"Ready?" she asked.

"Ready," KT said nervously.

"Right behind you, Kitten, let's bolt," said Jake.

Okay, no turning back now. Step 3 was about to begin.

Looking around one last time to make sure the coast was clear Ruthie said, "On three we go...one...two...three."

No sooner had she said three, Ruthie took off, Jake followed in a flash and little KT flew faster than she had ever flown in her life directly behind her friends. KT flew so fast, she flew right by Jake and almost flew into Ruthie.

"I don't think anyone saw us Kitten, we're cruisin' and in the clear," Jake said.

Ruthie hopped on the back left tail wing, while KT and Jake worked the rope around the plane's wing and Ruthie's chest. They had practiced this little routine so often during the past three days that the three friends could do it in their sleep. KT flew under and around one last time making a triple knot and Jake gave it four or five strong tugs to make sure Ruthie was tightly secured.

Ruthie looked up at the clock, 11: 57 a.m.

"You guys better get out of here," she said. "I only have one ticket for this flight and I don't want to see you guys get in trouble."

"Kitten, when you want to get out just tug on the rope right here," Jake said handing Ruthie the rope. "Don't pull it unless you are ready to go. You only have one chance. Got it?"

Ruthie nodded. She looked into Jake's eyes and Jake looked into hers. The two leaned into each other like they were going to kiss, but KT grabbed Jake by the back of his wing and said, "Let's go, we have to get out of here, this thing is starting to move."

"See you on the ground Kitten," Jake said as he gently tapped his wing to Ruthie's head. "Good luck and have fun."

"I will and thanks to both of you guys. I'll see you on the ground," said Ruthie.

KT and Jake flew off the plane's tail wing and found a quiet spot behind an abandoned luggage carrier on the airport tarmac. From their hiding spot they watched as their friend who was now strapped to the tail wing of flight G777 to London leave the runway and take off from the ground.

"There she goes," said KT.

"Yes, there she goes, there she goes to 37,901 feet, the easy way," said Jake.

"If that's the easy way, I don't want to see the hard way," said KT.

CHAPTER 22
Step 3

Taking off tied to the tail wing of a jumbo jet airplane was somewhat bumpier than Ruthie had thought it would be and quite a bit noisier. The rumbling of the jet engines and the planes tires on the runway combined to make one heck of a racket. Once off the ground things got much quieter. The wind picked up rather quickly. Ruthie was beginning to become quite cold sitting there on the top the plane's tail wing. She looked at her altimeter, which she had strapped to her right leg, it read 11,534. This was ten times higher than she had flown when she reached the top of the Empire State Building. She looked around and noticed she was above the few clouds that were in the sky. Directly below her she could see the greenish blue of the Atlantic Ocean. Behind her and to her left she could still see New York City with all its big buildings, including the Empire State Building. Beyond the great building she could see the green of Central Park and home. She wondered if she had made the right decision by not telling her family about Step 3. She quickly talked herself out of that idea and decided she had made the right choice. She was really enjoying her one way flight up.

Ruthie went over her plan about twenty three times in her head. It was simple. As soon as her prized altimeter read greater than 30,000, she would simply pull the rope as Jake had instructed her to, fall backwards spreading her wings as wide open as they could go, fall as far away from the plane as possible, and then float on back to the ground like a feather. 37,901 feet the easy way, as Jake had said.

Ruthie took another look at her altimeter 21,733 feet, only 10,000 more feet to go.

Back down on the ground, KT and Jake watched Ruthie take off. They saw her plane climb off into the distance and head out over the Atlantic Ocean. They stayed until both of them had lost sight of her plane.

"Not much more we can do now," Jake said. "Why don't we head home and wait there until Kitten, I mean, Ruthie, flies back home to Central Park."

This was the first time KT could remember that she had ever agreed with Jake. She had an uneasy feeling about this whole production from the beginning. From the top secret decision, to the ultra secret meetings, to Jake's involvement, to keeping Step 3 from Ruthie's mom and dad, to the potential for danger, KT didn't like it one bit. Step 3 couldn't be over soon enough for her. She just hoped Ruthie was okay up there all by herself.

Back on the tail wing at 26,461 feet, Ruthie was PERFECT, not Perfect Jen "perfect", but honest to goodness 100 percent on top of the world perfect. Ruthie couldn't believe how great she felt. She had never felt so happy or alive in her life. Her only regret was that she didn't have somebody else up there to share it with. She was amazed how well her body was handling the cold, the high winds and the thin air. She looked at the altimeter, 28,602 feet. She didn't want it to end!

Back in Central Park, KT was sitting in her room looking out the window searching the sky for any sign of Ruthie when her mother called her.

"KT honey, the phone is for you. It's Ruthie's dad. I think he's looking for Ruthie," said KT's mom.

"Hello," said KT to the bird on the other end of the phone.

"Hi KT, it's Mr. B, have you seen Ruthie? I haven't heard from her since she left this morning and I'm getting worried. It's Wednesday, you know, and I think she might be up to something," I said.

"No Mr. B, I haven't seen Ruthie since noon time," KT said keeping a promise she made to herself that she would not lie but still keep Ruthie secret. "Maybe she's with Jake."

"I bet you're right. She's been spending an awful lot of time with that boy lately and I don't like it." I said. "I'll have to do something about that. I'll call The Answer and see if I can get Jake's number."

"Okay Mr. B," said KT. "Good luck."

Up at 29,211 feet, Ruthie was getting ready to pull her rope and set herself free. It was getting pretty cold up there and it was extremely windy now. The plane was really moving fast and the wind was ruffling Ruthie's feathers. Ruthie could see her breath when she breathed and she was getting concerned about the worsening conditions. She looked down below and saw the sun bouncing off the greenish blue ocean. She looked down at her right leg, her altimeter read 30,085. It was time to pull the rope. It was time to fly home. She hoped she didn't have a long flight back. She wanted to share everything with Jake and KT. She hoped that her parents wouldn't be too angry. Everything was alright. Step 3 would be behind her and next Step would be Step 4, the attempt to break Ruppell Griffon's world record.

Pull the rope, Ruthie, she thought to herself, pull the rope and fall backwards away from the plane. She glanced at her altimeter, it read 30,523 feet. Ruthie took one last look around and pulled the rope. Nothing happened!

On the ground, I picked up the phone to call The Answer. "Hello Marty? This is Mr. B, just wondering if you've seen Ruthie or Jake today," I asked.

"You know Mr. B. I haven't seen much of either of them all week. I called Jake's earlier today but he wasn't there. His Grandma said he went off to the airport with that pretty little girl, so I just figured Ruthie and he took a fly out to the airport to watch the planes," said the Answer.

"The airport? Why would they fly out to the airport?"

"That's a question I don't have the answer to Mr. B. I'm sorry," said The Answer.

"That's okay, I know who just might. Thanks for your help. Good bye," I said hanging up the phone.

I held down the receiver and dialed KT's number. That little sparrow knew something she wasn't telling me.

Up at 31,011 feet, Ruthie pulled on her rope a second time, nothing happened. She pulled on the rope a third time and again nothing happened. She looked down at the rope and noticed that a layer of ice had formed on the knot freezing it. 31, 812 feet, Ruthie was starting to get nervous. Awful thoughts filled her head for a moment. She took a deep breath and regained her composure. She reached down with her wing and started to rub the rope knot as fast as she could. She hoped that the friction would chip off some of the ice melting enough of it so she could free herself. 32,444 feet,

Ruthie's rubbing seemed to be working but there was only one way to know for sure.

She pulled the rope.

Back home, I got KT on the phone. "Hello KT, Yes this is Mr. B. again," I said.

"Oh, hhhhiiii Mmmmr. Bbbb. Any luck finding Ruthie?" KT asked.

"Well an interesting thing KT, I spoke with Marty and he said that Ruthie and Jake went to the airport together earlier today. This wouldn't happen to have anything to do with Step 3 would it?" I said.

KT paused for a moment. How did he figure this out? Who knew? She knew she didn't say anything, The Answer didn't know, Jake must have told his Grandmother. She wasn't breaking any trust if she told him now. She didn't want to lie.

"Why would you ask something like that Mr. B.?" KT asked.

"Because today is Wednesday, because I know my little girl and because I don't trust that boy Jake," I said.

"Well Mr. B., she may have gone to the airport with Jake but it was Ruthie's idea not Jake's. I'm sure she'll be home soon," said KT.

"Where are they KT?" I asked.

"I think Jake's home by now but I'm not really sure where Ruthie is right now," said KT. "That's the truth"

"KT..." I said.

"Mr. B., I'm sorry I gave my word. I can't tell you. Remember what Ruthie said to us? Trust her," said KT.

"Trust her...it's getting harder and harder to trust that little girl each day," I said.

At 32,444 feet, Ruthie pulled the rope. She pulled it as hard as she could. The ice chipped away. The knot loosened. Ruthie prepared to finally leave the tail wing of the plane. She gave it another big yank, the rope knot was undone. She fell backward rolling six times. As she tumbled she spread her wings as wide as they could go. Ruthie righted herself and went into a controlled glide. She rolled up the piece of rope she had held on to and stuffed it in her wing. She looked up and saw the plane still climbing higher moving farther and farther away from her. She looked at her altimeter one last time, 31, 907 feet. She pressed the small circular RESET button on the altimeter locking it at zero. She turned back toward New York City and home.

Step 3 was complete. 37,901 and Griffon's record would have to wait until another day but for now 31,907 feet the "easy way" was feeling pretty good.

CHAPTER 23
Mommy! Daddy! I'm Home

Flying home was not as much fun as the flight up. Ruthie flew west toward the setting sun until she saw New York City in the distance. She was happy to see the familiar sights of home. She had a relatively easy flight down alternating between gliding downward and flapping her wings to slow her descent when she began to move too fast.

She was preparing to land on her branch when she noticed KT was waiting on their wall just below her tree. Ruthie pulled in for a landing on the wall near KT. KT was pacing back and forth with her head down and didn't even see Ruthie fly in.

"Hey you!" Ruthie said. "Nothing to worry about, I'm back and it went great. Had a little problem with the rope strap but everything is okay. It's all good."

"Good to hear, but it's not all good here. Your dad found out that you went to the airport with Jake and he's not too happy. He knows something is up. I don't think he knows everything about Step 3 but he's super mad. I think you are in big trouble," KT said.

"How'd he find out?" Ruthie asked.

"He hadn't seen or heard from you, realized it was Wednesday, got worried and started to call around. I spoke with him and told him nothing but he called Marty and Marty spilled the beans," KT said.

"How'd Marty know?" Ruthie asked.

"He didn't. Marty called Jake's looking for him and Jake's Grandmother told Marty that Jake went to the airport with you. Then Marty told your dad when your dad called him. I knew something like this was going to happen. I hate secrets," said KT.

"No big deal KT. Don't worry, it's over now, I'm all right and Step 3 is complete. I promise no more secrets. No more secrets," Ruthie said.

"Thanks. You'll have to tell me all about Step 3 later," KT said.

"I will. I'll tell everyone Friday night before the Incredible Hawk," said Ruthie. "I'll see you later. I've got to go see my mom and dad and see if I can calm them down. Hopefully they are not too angry with me."

Ruthie flew up to our branch and slowly opened the door to our home. My wife and I were sitting there waiting for our little pride and joy to come home.

"Mommy...Daddy...I'm home," Ruthie screamed running over giving each of us a big hug.

"Where have you been young lady? Your father and I have been worried sick" my wife said.

"Well that's an interesting question," Ruthie answered.

"You've been with that boy Jake, haven't you? What were you doing at the airport with THAT boy?" I questioned.

"Well, kind of," Ruthie said. "I was with him and KT for a little while."

"What do you mean kind of?" my wife asked.

"Mommy, Daddy, let's sit down. I have a story to tell you," Ruthie said.

Ruthie then proceeded to tell us all about the day's events. She outlined how KT, Jake and she met, made their way to the airport, how they strapped her to the tail wing of a jet airplane and how she flew to 30,000 feet on the wing of that plane before releasing herself and floating back home.

"Step 3 is complete," she finished. She then placed a piece of the rope that was holding her to the tail wing and an airline napkin that she had picked up off the ground before she took off on our kitchen table in front of us.

"These are for you," Ruthie said awaiting our approval.

Instead of congratulating her, we each paused for a moment.

"Are you okay?" asked my wife.

"I'm fine. Everything is okay," Ruthie answered.

"Good," I said.

I took a deep breath, paused again and looked at my wife. She gave me the nonverbal okay to let loose and then I did!

"How could you have taken such a risk without telling us!? How could you sneak around like that!? How could you worry us so much!? How could you possibly not trust US!?" I hollered. "You asked us to trust you, but you also need to trust us!"

"IIIII'mmmm sssorry," Ruthie said fighting back the tears. "I wasn't thinking. You're right. I didn't trust you while you have trusted me through this whole thing. I'm sorry, I'm very sorry. Everything is okay now. Step 3 is complete. I thought everything would be okay when I came through that door and said 'Mommy and Daddy I'm home' but I was wrong. It will never happen again. Like I told KT, no more secrets, I promise, no more secrets."

Ruthie gave each of us a real hug this time. The three of us spent the rest of the night talking, talking about the record and her friends. Our little girl was home, but the next seven days were going to be very interesting indeed.

CHAPTER 24
Not Your Typical Friday Night

Thursday morning Ruthie got up and made two phone calls, one to Jake and the other to her special guest to confirm her plans for Friday night.

"Okay, it's all set. I'll see you at my house at 7 p.m. sharp tomorrow night. Everyone will be here to watch the Incredible Hawk and I want to tell everyone then. See you tomorrow," Ruthie said to the voice of the other end of the phone. "Good bye."

"It's all set," Ruthie said to us.

"Good dear, I think everyone will really enjoy meeting your special visitor," said my wife.

Ruthie spent the remainder of the day around the house. KT and Perfect Jen both called to see if she wanted to play but Ruthie refused deciding instead to stay at home with us. I think she felt a tad guilty about not telling us about Step 3 before it happened. She spent most the day reading the Ruppell Griffon book we had purchased for her at the book signing event. Despite being only a few weeks old, Ruthie's book looked like it was twenty years old. That poor book had numerous dog eared pages and yellow highlighted lines marking out paragraphs and words that were important only to her.

Friday morning arrived and things seemed quite normal around our home. Ruthie made her usual calls to her friends confirming they were planning on attending the usual Friday night activities. Everyone confirmed including Jake and The Answer. I was especially glad to hear that The Answer was going to be here because I was sure I had a true stumper for him.

After dinner Ruthie retuned her Griffon book to her room, placing it on her bookshelf directly next to the box that contained her prized altimeter. The Mrs. and I prepared the snacks, making sure we put extra butter on the popcorn for Perfect Jen. The Mrs. wiped down each of the frames on the wall, the ones that contained all the mementos from Ruthie's first three steps. These prized positions now took up the entire back wall of our living room. I paused to watch my wife clean each of these frames and slowly realized that we were witnessing an impressive march toward an historic moment, the breaking of the Great Griffon's long standing world record.

Ruthie was more nervous than usual and started pacing back and forth between the kitchen and living room until the evening's first knock on the door.

"I'll get it!!! I'll get it!!!" Ruthie screeched as she ran for the door.

It was KT and Evan. Evan had a brand new Incredible Hawk costume on for the evening and KT was wearing a new purple ribbon in the feathers on the top of her head. The pair greeted Ruthie and made their way to their usual spots in the living room in front of the TV.

"Greeting and salutations fine citizens," Evan said to the Mrs. and me.

"Greeting and salutations fine citizen," we both responded simultaneously.

"Hey, Mr. and Mrs. B.," KT said to us, "hope you're both not too upset with me for not telling you about Step 3."

"Everything is okay with us honey," my wife said. "We straightened everything out the other night with Ruthie. There will be no more secrets in this house."

"That's good to hear," KT said. "I don't know if I can take another secret."

Perfect Jen and Backwards Bob arrived and exchanged their welcomes with everyone. Jake and The Answer soon followed. Everyone was in their favorite place and the show wasn't scheduled to start for another ten minutes.

"OK Marty...I mean The Answer...it's finally time for you to meet your match," I said. "I've been saving this one for a few weeks. I think I've got the ultimate stumper for you."

"Have at it Mr. B.," The Answer responded. "Give me your best shot. You know no one has been able to stump me yet."

I paused for a second or two to make sure everyone in the room was listening.

"Marty, what is the meaning of this string of characters – "**941s22a546f31e1t23y19653**," I asked.

Marty repeated the string and didn't respond with an answer. He asked for a piece of paper and a pencil to jot it down. I repeated it for him one more time. Everyone else in the room listened intensely.

"**941s22a546f31e1t23y19653**," I said again.

The Answer started to talk to himself, "It's not the ancient Apache Indian code and it doesn't match ancient Egyptian hieroglyphics. It can't be deciphered using Roman numerals or the Greek alphabet."

A few more minutes passed. There was absolute silence in the room until Evan cried out, "I've got it! I have the answer! I solved it before The Answer!"

Evan walked over to me and whispered his answer to me in my left ear.

"Very good son, you are correct. Looks like little Evan here beat you to it Marty," I said.

Like popping popcorn, the kids in the room each came to the answer themselves within a few seconds, everyone that is except The Answer. The fact that all his friends solved the riddle before him was driving him crazy. He continued scribbling calculations. He was on his third piece of paper, crumbling the other two in balls and tossing them to the floor, but he still couldn't solve the riddle.

"mih llet t'noD" (Don't tell him) urged Backwards Bob to his friends as The Answer continued to struggled to solve the problem.

"What'd he say," my wife asked? "What that boy says is always the biggest riddle to me."

Everyone laughed.

Ruthie glanced at the clock and noticed it was one minute until 7 p.m. She stood up from her spot in front of the TV and proclaimed, "You have one more minute, Marty. You have until 7 p.m. and then you are done."

Just then there was a knock on the front door. My wife got up to answer the door.

"I think your guest has arrived," I said to Ruthie.

"Guest, what guest? We are all here, even Jake," said Perfect Jen giving a little grin and wink to Jake. Ruthie noticed this little move by Perfect Jen and was not too happy with her. You could have shot lasers out of Ruthie's eyes. She was quite upset.

"I've invited a special guest here tonight," Ruthie said. "We are not going to be watching the Incredible Hawk tonight. I have a special announcement to make and I want to share it with all my best friends and family tonight. I've invited a special guest to share this announcement with us as well."

There was a gasp of disbelief by everyone in the room. Who was this special guest and what was so important that Ruthie would turn off the Incredible Hawk?

"Marty, you have ten more seconds," Ruthie said.

The entire room started to count down...

"9...8...7...6...5...4..."

The Answer frantically scribbled even more calculations down on his paper.

"3...2...1!"

"I give up guys," the Answer said. "You win Mr. B. I hate to admit it but you've stumped me, you've finally beaten The

Answer! Now tell what's the answer to the riddle **941s22a546f31e1t23y19653**? It is driving me insane."

"Tell him Evan, you solved it first," I said.

"The answer is, **THERE IS SAFETY IN NUMBERS**. Get it, 941s22a546f31e1t23y19653, S—A---F—E---T—Y in numbers!" Evan said.

Everyone in the room laughed including The Answer. The kids quickly turned their attention toward Ruthie when Perfect Jen exclaimed "Enough of these stupid riddles. Who's this special guest, Penguin? What's this big announcement already?"

"Thank you, Perfect Jen. I want to thank all of you for helping me get this far in my quest to break the Great Griffon's world record. Steps 1, 2 and 3 are now complete and I've asked my special guest here to help me with Step 4," Ruthie said.

"Step 3, Penguin?" Perfect Jen asked. "Did I miss something? When was Step 3?"

"Sorry, more on that in a moment friends. For now I'd like to bring in our special guest. He's agreed to help me with Step 4. He has agreed to help me break the record. Mom, can you please escort him in?" Ruthie said.

He walked in through our living room arch and the entire room gasped in awe. They then broke out into spontaneous applause. The giant bird gave a bow, nodded his head in thanks and waved his wing signaling the room to please stop. Ruppell Griffon, The Legend, was in the room.

"Thank you so much kids for your warm welcome," he bellowed in his perfect tone, "but tonight is young Ruthie's night and I am only here on her behalf. I am here to support her and make sure she is successful in her record breaking attempt. Miss Ruthie the floor is yours."

Ruthie thanked Griffon then told her friends about the previous week's events. She outlined how KT, Jake and she laid out the plans for Step 3. She explained how they secretly made their way to the airport, how Jake and KT tied her to the plane's tail wing, how the rope froze from the ice, how she freed herself and how she glided back home to Central Park. She made sure she mentioned how this never would have been possible without the help of KT and thanked her newest friend Jake (while being certain she was looking straight at Perfect Jen every time she mentioned Jake's name). She left nothing out except the fact that we were furious with her and that there would be no more secrets in our family. I had heard Ruthie's story a few times now but it was still nice to hear her tell it again.

Ruthie finished her story. "I'm sure you all have questions about Step 3, but for now Step 3 is over and Step 4, the flight for the record, is my focus, our focus. Step 4, the record attempt, will happen this Wednesday," she said.

"yadsendeW sihT (This Wednesday?)," said Backwards Bob.

"Yes, this Wednesday," Ruthie said, "and you all have a special job, that is if you want it."

Each of the gang said yes including Perfect Jen.

"Good. Perfect Jen, since you were so good at it last time, you are in charge of publicity. Your job is to call the newspapers and TV stations and make sure they are all there."

"You got it Penguin, I'm on it. That's the perfect job for me," Perfect Jen said.

"Evan, you and Backwards Bob are in charge of security. Both of you have to make sure any crowd we have at the takeoff spot stays back so I have a clear spot to begin my flight," said Ruthie.

"For the protection of all who are good and bright in this world, the Incredible Hawk will be there," said Evan in his Incredible Hawk voice.

"oot eM (Me too) oot eM (Me too)," said Backward Bob.

"Marty, I'd like you to be in charge of weather reports. I'm going to need daily updates and hourly weather readings right up until takeoff," Ruthie said.

"I'm on it chief," said The Answer.

"Jake, my friend, I'd like you to be my practice buddy. I'm going to need someone to fly with and practice with this week and I'd like you to lend me a helping wing," Ruthie said.

"Sounds like a plan Kitten. I told you when we first met I'm here for you, whatever you need," Jake said.

"KT, you have a very special job. I want you to be my second in charge. I'd like you to help keep everyone in line. I want you to make sure everyone is doing their job and I want you to be the first bird to meet me when I land," Ruthie said.

KT got up and gave Ruthie a big hug and said, "I'm honored. I believe in you. Let's do this."

"Mommy and Daddy, you have the hardest job of anyone. I asked you when I first started this to trust me. Now when I'm tackling my biggest challenge I ask you yet again to trust me one more time," Ruthie said.

"We do honey, we do trust you," we both said fighting back our tears.

"That leaves one last bird without a job," Ruthie said. "Mr. Griffon, you've been my biggest inspiration through this entire journey. You've provided guidance in your words and actions, you've shown kindness with your generous gift, now I ask you if you would do me the honor of being my wingbird on Wednesday when I make my flight," Ruthie said turning to the legend. "I want you to make this flight with me."

"I am an old bird, Ruthie, but it will be my pleasure to fly with you. I will do the best these old wings can do. I will fly with you as high as I possibly can fly," Griffon said.

The entire room once again roared and applauded. They all started chanting "Ruthie!!! Ruthie!!!" Ruthie raised her wing like Griffon had done earlier and quieted her friends down.

"Thank you all. I love you. Takeoff is Wednesday at 12 noon. I'll be leaving from our wall right here in Central Park exactly at 12 noon on Wednesday. You all have very important jobs and I thank you."

The room quickly emptied. Griffon left first, the remainder of her friends followed the giant bird. The Answer was the last one to leave.

"Not your typical Friday night, hey Mr. B.," The Answer said "Not your typical Friday night."

CHAPTER 25
The Hardest Job of All

The next four days were a whirlwind of activity. Everyone had their jobs to do and they all worked very hard doing it.

Ruthie practiced and practiced. Much to Perfect Jen's and my disappointment, Jake was at her side every step of the way. Perfect Jen alerted all the press. NBC and ABC both sent camera crews and reporters over to interview Ruthie before the flight and the *Daily Bird Call* sent over a reporter every day. KT controlled all media access to Ruthie, granting only the shortest of meetings to everyone.

Evan and Backwards Bob roped off a takeoff area at the far corner of their wall to mark off the takeoff zone. KT instructed them to set off a special viewing area for her friends and us. The Answer had two TV's tuned to different weather stations at all times and had set up a network of instruments to monitor temperature, wind speed and pressure. He even went so far as to launch helium balloons every three hours equipped with tiny thermometers and radio antennas to take measurements as high up as possible. The Answer made sure to call KT every hour with the new readings and updates.

Ruppell Griffon did the best he could to stretch his creaky old bones and even took a few test flights. Griffon made sure to call Ruthie every night and upon Ruthie's request, even made certain he checked in with KT every night as well.

Things were taking hold and everything appeared to be in place for the big flight.

The Mrs. and I just sat there watching this entire production unfold before our eyes. We worried that our little girl may have bitten off more than she could chew. Ruthie was correct. We had the hardest job of all.

Tomorrow would be Wednesday and we were all ready for the record attempt. The question was, "Was Ruthie ready?"

CHAPTER 26
Step 4 – Birth of the Legend

Ruth awoke at approximately 7 a.m. as she usually did and greeted us at the breakfast table. She sat down for her usual corn muffin. She didn't appear nervous or anxious in the least. If we didn't know what lay ahead for her we'd have thought it was just another ordinary Wednesday.

"I've got to give KT a call to check on how things are going," Ruthie said. "I'm thinking we should head down around 11:30 a.m., I'll say a few words to the crowd before takeoff and then off we go."

"Sounds great dear," said the Mrs.

"Yes, sounds like a plan," I said.

Ruth got up from her chair and wiped the crumbs from her feathers. She strolled over to the phone and dialed KT's number.

"Hello KT it's me, Ruthie. How are things going? Good…..nice…..Did the Answer call in with the weather report?..Every hour, that's good….Sounds like good flying weather to me….Are you keeping Perfect Jen busy with the press….Perfect..OK…. Meet me here at eleven and please tell everyone else to be at the viewing area on the wall by 11:30, we takeoff right at noon….Thanks KT….See you soon, bye." Ruthie said hanging up the phone.

"We are all set. KT's coming over at eleven to go over any final matters and then we'll meet the gang on the wall at 11:30. Think anyone else will come to watch me takeoff?" Ruthie asked.

"Will anyone come you ask? Are you crazy," I said holding up the morning paper. "You've been front page news for the last four days. NBC and ABC are covering your flight LIVE. We'll be lucky to get down to the wall without being mobbed. You're big news right now sweetie, big news!"

Ruthie had been so absorbed with the preparation and training that she didn't realize how popular she had become. In her mind she was still just a little girl who loved to fly, but in everyone else's mind she had become a little girl who was trying to break the unbreakable record. She had become a hero.

At precisely 11:00 a.m. Ruthie met KT at our front door. They scurried into Ruthie's room to go over the final details.

"The boys are set with security, the press is already at the wall waiting for you and I spoke with Mr. Griffon. He said he'll be there precisely at 11:30. The Answer has been calling me every hour with weather updates. Temperature, pressure and wind conditions are perfect. He said remember to watch out for icing when you get above 25,000 feet. You are ready to go kid! The world record is yours, go get it," KT said.

"Thanks for everything. It might get crazy out there but remember I'll be thinking of you. You were the one who always believed in me," Ruthie said. "I'm ready, let's do this."

Ruthie got up from the floor, where she and KT had been sitting, and started to walk out of the room.

"Hold it…hold it…you can't go anywhere without this," KT said grabbing Griffon's altimeter off Ruthie's bed where it had been laying.

"Make sure you press this," KT said pressing the RESET button. The prized altimeter now read **0**.

The two friends walked off and the Mrs. and I joined them. It was now 11:42 a.m. Ruthie was late.

It was an utter mob scene down at the wall and all around Central Park. There were birds sitting on every free branch, every telephone wire and every speck of grass adjacent to the wall. Ruppell Griffon and Ruthie's friends were in a roped off area next to the takeoff spot that Evan and Backwards Bob had created. There were TV cameras everywhere and flashes from cameras continued to go off as Ruthie and the three of us flew down and made our way to the wall. After we landed, the three of us made our way to the viewing section while Ruthie joined Griffon in the takeoff area.

Griffon began to speak as the TV cameras focused on him.

"We are about to witness an historic feat today by a truly remarkable young girl. We are about to witness the birth of a legend," Griffon said in his usually classy manner.

Ruthie stepped in front of Griffon and said, "Thank you all for coming today. I am honored and humbled. I would not be here without the support of my family and many friends. I thank you all for your love, trust and loyalty."

Ruthie blew a kiss to us in the viewing area, gave a little nod to KT and a special wink to Jake. She said a few words to Griffon that only he could hear. The bell tower clock struck twelve noon.

"Up and away!" Ruthie said mimicking the Incredible Hawk. Off she went, straight up like a bullet shot out of a gun. The Great Griffon quickly followed her. Griffon was impressed with how fast she was. It took Griffon a few minutes longer than he thought to catch up to Ruthie. The two had never flown together and they were both enjoying each others company on the way up. They spoke about Griffon's record flight back in '75 and about all the attention and interest that surrounded Ruthie's quest to break his record.

"10,722 feet," Ruthie said looking at her altimeter. "How you doing you old bird?" she said to Griffon playfully.

"Hanging in there," Griffon said. He was growing increasing tired but he wanted to support Ruthie as long as he could. "These old wings are holding up."

"Looking good so far," Ruthie said. "Wind conditions are fine. Not too cold. I'm feeling pretty good myself."

All the practice and training were paying off for Ruthie. Her preparation, Steps 1, 2 and 3, Griffon's advice and guidance, everything was helping make today's flight perfect.

The pair continued to climb upwards. The higher they got the less talkative Griffon became. Ruthie began to worry as they approached 20,000 feet.

"Are you okay?" Ruthie asked to Griffon as she looked over at him and noticed he was beginning to wobble. The higher they flew the less steady he became.

"I think it's time, Mr. Griffon. You've done more than enough," Ruthie said.

"I agree little one. I'm done. I'm afraid you are going to have to do the last leg of the flight on your own," Griffon said.

"Go. Go back and tell them that everything is okay. I'm fine. Tell them I'm going to go break the record today," Ruthie said.

Griffon stopped his climb and leveled off. He continued to watch Ruthie as she flew higher and higher. He watched her until she was just a small speck in the summer sky.

Griffon turned and floated back down to Central Park. He spotted the landing area. He would go and deliver his message to the waiting crowd.

Ruthie had now risen to 28,333 feet. She noticed the wind speed had increased considerably and that it was getting harder and harder to climb. The icing concerns, that had bothered her on the plane in Step 3, were of no worry. It was certainly getting colder but Ruthie was not feeling any ill effects.

It was quiet up here, Ruthie thought, quieter than when she was on the plane. With no one to talk to, she thought about everything that had happened since that 4th of July night when she first flew. She thought about her friends, she thought about Sully and Old Yellow, she thought about Jake. She thought about the Empire State Building and the Incredible Hawk. She looked at her altimeter 32,455 feet. She was almost there only 5,446 feet to go to break Griffon's record, the world record.

Back on the ground, after an agonizing two and half hours, The Great Griffon was spotted by the remaining crowd. Little Evan was the first to see him as he was coming in for his final descent.

"Look there he is. It is the Incredible Hawk," Evan said in his normal voice. "He's coming! He's coming!!"

The Answer grabbed his binoculars and zeroed in on the figure.

"That's not the Incredible Hawk silly, that's Mr. Griffon," The Answer said. "I don't see Ruthie however."

The crowd of birds that had gathered at the beginning of the day had dwindled down to approximately fifty or so loyal supporters. Both TV stations were still there broadcasting and the *Daily Bird Call* still had a photographer and reporter on hand. Evan and Backwards Bob, along with Jake, had set up machines full of multicolored confetti that they planned to set off when Ruthie finally landed.

The Great Griffon sailed in for his landing. The old legend was a tad wobbly on his approach but he was still an impressive figure as he came in for a landing. He stretched out his wings as far as he could, so wide that he blocked out the sun. He came in attempting to make a gentle landing. He lost his balance for a brief moment however, but soon righted himself. He looked down and to the left searching for the family viewing section, for the Mrs. and me. He did not spot us immediately because we had move to Ruthie's takeoff area. Griffon turned his head in our direction and spotted us a moment later. The great bird gave each of us a wink and the okay sign. We knew Ruthie was fine.

"Young Ruthie is moments away from returning friends," Griffon said in a loud bellowing tone, to the remaining crowd. "It appears that she is going to break my record. She was healthy and in good spirits when we parted. We will only know for sure when she returns with the altimeter if she has indeed broken my record."

Up near 37,000 feet, Ruthie was not the least bit concerned as she approached the record height. She wanted to be careful to fly only one foot higher. She glanced at the altimeter, 36,902 feet. She had less than 100 feet to go. She began to think of Ruppell Griffon, how great he was and how she hoped that she would be just like him when some young bird was attempting to break her new record.

Ruthie was now focusing on just two things, the altimeter that was strapped around her wing and the spot twenty five feet away where she was imagining a finish line. The altimeter now read 37,876. Just about there. No obstacle, no airplanes, nothing but clear blue skies. Ruthie thought about what Jake had said about Step 3, "37,901 feet the easy way". He was wrong, this was the easy way. Step 3 was anything but easy.

37,897...37,898...37,899...37,900...37,901!!!! The record was officially broken. Ruthie had done it!

There was no fanfare, no bells went off, there wasn't any confetti shot into the air. That would all have to wait until Ruthie made it back home. Ruthie leveled off and hung in the air for a moment. She reached into her wing and pulled out the envelope Ruppell Griffon had given her that night at her house when he had given her the altimeter. She opened it and pulled out a feather. It was one of Griffon's feathers. Griffon told Ruthie he wanted to get back to 37,900 feet and this was the only way he could. Ruthie released the feather. It took off in the wind floating up even higher. Ruthie watched it float away and smiled. "We made it Mr. Griffon. We made it." She looked around and noticed it didn't look any different than when she was 1,000 feet high. She hit the button on the altimeter to lock it into place. She didn't want it to start going backwards as she descended. She wanted to prove to her friends and family that she indeed did break the record.

Back on the ground, ten minutes had past and there was no sign of Ruthie, twenty minutes and still no sign. We all were scanning the sky looking for her but we saw nothing. The bell tower clock bell rang three bells for three o'clock. No Ruthie! Thirty minutes had elapsed since Griffon landed, we were getting worried. Just as the clock rang its third bell Perfect Jen exclaimed "I see her, right over there," pointing off in the far distance over a block of buildings.

"It is her," The Answer said. "She is coming!" he cried to the crowd.

"Make sure you get this. She's right there. Make sure you get her landing. Make sure you get her with Griffon. Don't miss her hugging her parents," NBC reporter Buzzard Scott said to his camera bird.

"On three bring the camera on me...1...2...3...This is Buzzard Scott live in Central Park where little Ruthie B. Goose, the little girl that has captured everyone's attention with her world record chasing exploits, is about to land ending what could be a record setting flight. Her family, friends and loyal fans have gathered to greet her and hopefully celebrate her magnificent feat. You'll notice she's just about twenty five feet from landing. Here she comes spreading those beautiful wings, stretching out her yellow feet and coming in for text book landing inches from where she took off just three short hours ago."

The Mrs. and I ran over and gave her a big hug. She gave us the biggest hug she had ever given us and whispered "thanks" to both of us. Evan and Backwards Bob waited for the signal to set off the confetti machines. Perfect Jen just stood in a perfect pose hoping the TV cameras got her best side. The Answer and KT stood in front of Ruthie waiting anxiously for her to say if she broke the record. Jake was off in the corner helping Evan and Backwards Bob with the confetti machines. Ruppell Griffon spoke for all us.

"Well, young Ruthie do we have a new legend?" Griffon asked.

Ruthie waited for what seemed to be 100 million minutes but was really only about ten seconds. She simply held up Griffon's altimeter as high as she could for everyone to see.

37,901

Backwards Bob and Evan set off the confetti machines. Confetti of every color shot into the air from every direction. Griffon picked up Ruthie and held her high in the air for all to see. KT and The Answer hugged, jumped up and down and then flew up so Ruthie could see them. Jake was mobbed by the remaining crowd and was unable to reach the landing zone. The Mrs. and I stood by Perfect Jen with our wings on her shoulders. The two of us watched with pride and joy. We felt relief that this was finally over. The rest of the crowd mobbed Ruthie and chanted her name. Word quickly got out that the world record had been broken. Thousands of birds ascended on Central Park and the wall.

The celebrations lasted for about sixty minutes. The TV cameras finally shut off, the newspaper reporters finally left and the mob of supporters and fans made their last cheer. The Answer packed up all his instruments and left with KT. They were both happy for their friend and proud of the role they played. Perfect Jen left with Backwards Bob directly behind her. The Great Ruppell Griffon left with Evan, the little boy in the Incredible Hawk costume. They made an interesting pair.

The Mrs. left just before me to get Ruthie's bed ready. Our little girl was tired. It had been a long exciting adventure.

And I left with my little girl, the new legend, resting on my back, giving her one last ride on "Air Dad". It was time to put the new legend to bed. It had been a very long day for all of us, but I have to admit it was extremely fun watching the birth of the legend.

CHAPTER 27-The Epilog
Something to Tell KT

Ruthie got up at 5:43 a.m. the next morning. She really didn't sleep the previous night, she was too excited. She was now a world record holder and, as Ruppell Griffon said, a new legend.

Ruthie quietly walked across our hallway floor and opened the front door slowly, trying not to wake either of us. She made her way out on to the main branch of our tree and looked down at the wall. The sun was beginning to rise in the eastern sky but it was still dark enough to make it seem like night time. There were all sorts of different colored confetti strewn over the wall. The viewing area setup for the family was still up, but the ropes around her takeoff area were now on the ground having been knocked down by the fans that mobbed Ruthie upon her arrival.

Ruthie glanced down and noticed a lone figure scrounging around for souvenirs down on the wall. She decided to fly down to see if anyone else was down there.

"What are you doing here so early in the morning?" Ruthie asked as she landed on the wall.

"Oh, hi Kitten," Jake said a bit surprised to see his friend. "I'm just getting a few souvenirs for my Grandma. She couldn't be here yesterday, but she watched it all on TV. She's a big fan."

"Souvenirs for Grandma, hmm?" she said questioning Jake. "Maybe she'd like one of these," she said pulling a feather from her wing.

She began to reach out to hand the feather to him.

Reaching for the feather Jake tripped on some confetti and fell into Ruthie's out stretched wings. Ruthie wrapped her wings around Jake catching him so he wouldn't fall.

"Nice catch, Kitten" Jake said looking into Ruthie's eyes.

Before Ruthie could respond, Jake leaned into Ruthie and planted a big kiss right on Ruthie's beak. Ruthie didn't pull away, surprising herself she kissed back.

"What did you do that for?" Ruthie asked Jake.

"I guess I just wanted to know what it was like to kiss a legend," Jake said.

Ruthie released Jake from her grip and handed Jake her feather. She then turned and started to fly back to her home without saying a word.

"Where are you going Kitten?" Jake asked.

"I'm going to call KT. I've got to tell her something!" Ruthie yelled back to Jake as she flew off. "I've really got to tell her something," she said again loud enough that only she could hear.

The Glossary
(or what was the meaning of that word?)

Altimeter- Is a device that measures how high an object is. Balloons, helicopters and airplanes all are equipped with altimeters.

Avierica – (from Aviary and America) "The world of Birds in the United States," as in *Good Morning Avierica*.

Buzzard Scott – The most popular weather bird and newscaster on NBC (National Bird Channel. Buzzard Scott can be seen every morning forecasting the weather and every night with special news reports.

Chickalodean – Channel 21 on your TV. It's the most popular TV network for young birds. The Incredible Hawk is shown every Friday night from 7 p.m. – 8:00 p.m.

Invasion- A large scale onslaught usually associated with armies and war.

Impression-A mark left by an object or a feeling left by a person or place left in one's mind.

Injustice- A wrong or unfair act perpetrated against a person by a group of people, government or criminal.

Madison Square Garden – The most famous sporting arena located in New York City. It is home to the New York Knicks National Basketball Team and New York Rangers National Hockey League team.

Momentous-A very special or important moment in time.

Mount Everest- Mt. Everest is the world's tallest mountain, located in Nepal is Central Asia. Mt. Everest's peak is 29,029 feet high.

Observation Deck- A room or area near or at the top of high buildings, usually surrounded by large windows, where people go to look out and view the surrounding sites.

Palindrome- A word or phrase that is spelled the exact same forwards or backwards. The most famous palindrome from literature and history is "Able was I ere I saw Elba," said by Napoleon Bonaparte while in exile on the Island of Elba.

Tri-state Area – Three states make up the New York City tri-state area, New York, New Jersey and Connecticut.

Unremitting – Never ending, continual.

That's the Fact –
Fun True Facts about Things in this Book

- **The Bar-Headed Goose** – (Ruthie B. Goose and her family) can fly over 50 miles an hour on their own power, add the thrust of tailwinds they are able to reach speeds of up to 100 miles an hour.

The same powerful and unremitting flapping that helps propel them over the mountains also generates body heat, which is retained by their down feathers. This heat, in turn, helps keep ice from building up on their wings.

(Source: M.R. Fedde, an emeritus professor of anatomy and physiology at Kansas State University's School of Veterinary Medicine)

- **Bar-Headed Geese** have been seen as high as 33,382 feet. This bird, which breeds in Central Asia, migrates through the Himalayan range. In addition, they have recently been seen throughout England (probably as a result of escaped geese that were people pets)

- The highest-flying bird ever recorded was a **Ruppell griffon**, a vulture with a wingspan of about 10 feet. On November 29, 1975, a Ruppell griffon was sucked into a jet engine 37,900 feet above the Ivory Coast. This altitude is more than a mile and a half higher than the summit of Mount Everest. The plane was damaged, though it landed safely.

(Source: The Audubon Magazine, "The High Life" by Lily Whiteman)

- In 1924 a **yellow-billed chough**, a crow-like bird that's among the highest-nesting species, followed a climbing expedition's food scraps to 26,500 feet on Everest. The avian altitude record in North America is held by a mallard, which collided with an airplane on July 9, 1963, at 21,000 feet above Elko, Nevada.

(Source: The Audubon Magazine, "The High Life", by Lily Whiteman)

- The **Empire State Building** built in 1930 at a cost of $24,700.00, is New York City's tallest building. It measures 1,454 feet (1,453 feet, 8 9/16th inches) to top of lightning rod and has 102 stories or floors.

The Building has 73 elevators. It is possible to ride from the lobby to the 86th floor in less than one minute.

During the spring and autumn, bird migration season, the lights that illuminate the Building tower are turned off on foggy nights. This is done so that the lights shining through the fog will not confuse birds, causing them to fly into the building.

(Source: www.esbny.com)

- **Central Park** – Created in 1853, Central Park was the first landscaped public park in the

United States. Central Park covers 843 acres, which is 6% of Manhattan. No tree can be higher than 350 ft tall in the park.

Summit Rock, on the western edge of Central Park at 83rd St., is the highest elevation in the park. It is 137 ½ feet, just a few feet above Vista Rock, home of Belvedere Castle.

(Source: www.centralpark.com)

- ***How high do most commercial air planes fly?*** The altitude of flight depends on the type of aircraft and the weather. Some run at 33,000 feet and some fly higher. Most commercial jets fly between 30,000-50,000 feet.

(Source: http://www.allstar.fiu.edu/aero/faq_princ_flight2.htm #altitude)

- Here's a list of words Backwards Bob would love. They are palindrome, which means they are spelled the same forwards as well as backwards

- Bob
- civic
- eye
- deed
- deified
- Hannah
- kayak
- level
- madam
- minim
- nun
- Otto

- racecar
- radar
- redder
- refer
- repaper
- reviver
- rotator
- rotor
- solos
- stats
- toot
- test set

(Source: http://www.rinkworks.com/words/palindromes.shtml)

- Elvis Presley was an American music and film icon who rose to popularity in the late 1950's. Known as "King of Rock and Roll" because he was one of the music industries first true superstars, Elvis remains today one of the highest selling recording artists of all time. In his early years, Elvis' trademark jet black hair and boyish good looks made him a favorite of young girls everywhere.

- There are 5,280 feet in a mile

- There are 12 inches in one foot

The Characters

- **Ruthie B. Goose:** Ruthie B. is the main character of our story. She is a young Bar-Headed goose who lives in an oak tree in New York City's Central Park with her mother and father. Like her parents, she is snow grey with black bars around her neck, yellow legs and yellow webbed feet. Her best friend is a little sparrow named KT. She has a group of close friends including KT, the Answer, Perfect Jen, Backwards Bob, and Evan. She also has a very special friend named Jake who she secretly has a crush on. Her two biggest loves are flying high and the Incredible Hawk television show. She is very stubborn, determined and loyal.

- **Mr. B. Goose (Dad and Narrator):** Mr. B. is the narrator of our story. He is a supportive dad and enjoys hanging out with Ruthie and her friends. He likes to try to stump the Answer with trivia facts and brain teasers, but doesn't have much luck. He secretly enjoys watching the *High Flying Adventures of the Incredible Hawk* with the kids.

- **Mrs. B. Goose (Mom and Mrs.):** Mrs. B. is a loving supportive mother and wife. She doesn't enjoy the Incredible Hawk, doesn't like or trust Perfect Jen and can never understand Backwards Bob. Her inability to understand Backward Bob drives her crazy.

- **KT:** She is a tiny little sparrow with a tiny little voice. She's a bit shy but at times can be quite spunky. She is Ruthie's best friend and loves her very much. She's also a big Incredible Hawk fan and thinks The Answer is perfect. She has a small crush on him. He doesn't have the slightest clue. She enjoys spending time with Evan and likes to protect him.

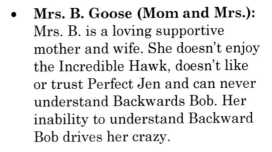

- **Marty "The Answer" Beckman:** He is a gangly seagull with an extra long neck. He's not the best looking bird on the block, but he is certainly the smartest. He's the oldest of Ruthie's friends. His best friend, outside of the group, is Jake. He introduces Ruthie and the gang to Jake. He doesn't like to be the center of attention, but he does like to have everyone know he is the smartest bird in the room. He enjoys frustrating Mr. B. and likes that Ruthie turns to him for answers.

- **Perfect Jen:** She is a perfect red cardinal. She's beautiful, speaks perfectly and never makes a mistake. She enjoys teasing Ruthie and loves that she can get under her skin. Her best friend is Backwards Bob. She's secretly jealous of Ruthie.

- **Backwards Bob:** He is a backwards talking spotted mallard (a duck). He hangs with Perfect Jen because she does all the talking. He feels sorry for her because the rest of the gang doesn't really care that much for her. He likes Ruthie, the Answer, KT and Evan because they treat him like any other bird, even though he talks backwards. He secretly likes that Mrs. B. can't understand anything he says.

- **Evan (The Incredible Hawk Boy):** The youngest of Ruthie's friends, Evan is a young hawk. Evan is always dressed in an Incredible Hawk costume. He always seems to be showing up in a new costume. No one really knows how many he owns. Evan is like everyone's younger brother. He usually speaks in an Incredible Hawk voice and believes the Incredible Hawk is real. He's a little overweight, always lags behind and is very lovable.

- **Jake:** Jake is COOL. He's a bit older than the rest of the gang and is more experienced than them. He's a yellow-billed cough, a crow like bird. Jake is all black with a yellow bill and red legs and feet. He has a permanent sneer that makes him look like a young Elvis Presley.

- **The Incredible Hawk:** Fast, strong, humble and kind, he is a true Super Hero. He is a fictional character and star of the Friday Night *Chickalodean*'s TV show *The Adventures of the Incredible Hawk*. From his secret lair high atop the Empire State Building, the Incredible Hawk fights crime and injustice in New York City. For the last two years his one hour show has been the highest rated show on Bird TV. He is idolized by young birds throughout the world. Ruthie's entire gang meets every Friday night at Ruthie's house to watch a new episode.

- **Ruppell Griffon:** The legend is the world record holder and author of the book , *Ruppell Griffon-A True Hero.* Griffon is a giant older vulture-like bird that stands 3 feet tall and has a wing span of over 8 feet wide. Griffon set his world record on November 29th, 1975 over the Ivory Coast in West Africa, when he flew to the record height of 37,900 feet. His is the record Ruthie must beat.

About the Authors & CMT

Ruthie Baker is a 10 year old 4th grader from Wilmington, MA. She enjoys swimming and playing video games. She plays the clarinet. She loves playing with her older brother, Andrew, and her dog, Razzle. This is her first published novel.

You can contact Ruthie at: ruthie@ruthiebgoose.com

Jeff Baker is also resident of Wilmington, MA. He is a graduate of Peabody High School and the University of Massachusetts-Amherst. He is a Marketing Manager at a manufacturing company in Malden, MA. This is his first published novel.

Jeff can be reached at jeff@ruthiebgoose.com

Charcot-Marie-Tooth (CMT) disorder is one of the most common inherited neurological disorders, affecting approximately 1 in 2,500 people in the United States. The condition is named for the three physicians who first identified it in 1886 - Jean-Martin Charcot and Pierre Marie in Paris, France, and Howard Henry Tooth in Cambridge, England. CMT, also known as hereditary motor and sensory neuropathy (HMSN) or peroneal muscular atrophy, comprises a group of disorders that affect peripheral nerves. The peripheral nerves lie outside the brain and spinal cord and supply the muscles and sensory organs in the limbs. Disorders that affect the peripheral nerves are called peripheral neuropathies.

To learn more about CMT visit: www.mda.org

About the Illustrator

Dan Gibson Born and raised in Vancouver, British Columbia Canada, Dan has been a professional freelance cartoonist over 25 years. Dan's cartoons and illustrations have been featured in dozens of books and magazines including Woman's Day, Variety and the National Enquirer.

Dan can be reached at www.dailycartoons.com

Online

Visit our website at **www.ruthiebgoose.com** to learn more about this book, purchase your very own Ruthie B. Goose and Incredible Hawk t-shirts, friend us on Facebook and find out about our book signing appearances.

Email us your comments and questions at ruthie@ruthiebgoose.com